# ROOM 21: PLAYTHING FOR THE MAFIA

## THE MAFIA

### CLUB SIN CHICAGO

MIKA LANE

HEADLANDS PUBLISHING

# GET A FREE BOOK

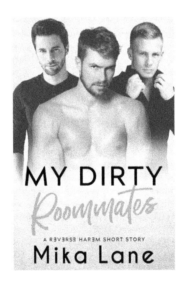

<u>My Dirty Roommates</u>

*When my three sexy roommates agree to help me as long as I do whatever they ask...I can't say no.*

The last thing I expect when I take a job in a new town is to end up living with three smoking hot roommates. Who also happen to be personal trainers. They are so out of my league, and I am so out of my element. But I can't afford to live alone in San Francisco, so have resigned myself to sharing.

Apparently, these guys like to share too…
Overhearing them say I'm cute gives me a nice ego boost. But I want to get in shape, and they'll only help me under one condition…
I have to do *whatever* they tell me to, *whenever* they tell me to do it. Instead of scaring me, the thought of being at their
beck and call sounds hot. And once they start with their naughty demands, I want them to never stop. They work me hard in the gym and everywhere else.

This whole roommate situation just put a new spin on 'sharing.'

# COPYRIGHT

**<u>Like deals and other cool stuff?</u>**
**<u>Sign up for my newsletter!</u>**

**I'm a maid at a sex club...**
Not exactly what I had in mind when I came to the
big city for college.
If my parents knew, they'd say I'm selling my soul
to the devil himself.
But it's nothing that should taint my soul.
Until it... does.

In a case of mistaken identity, I end up the favorite plaything for three very handsome, powerful men.

Possessive, passionate, and dominating…. both inside the club and out.

Only the fantasy scenarios we act out are nothing compared to the rush I get when I learn who they really are.

They're mobbed up.

And they want me to be theirs…

# AUTHOR'S NOTE

Club Sin Room Twenty-One: Plaything for the Mafia contains the following mature themes:

- Virgin heroine
- Roleplay
- Sex club

- Spanking
- Somnophilia
- Three hot mafia dudes
- Escaping religious repression
- Reverse harem
- Page turning sexy times

18+. Please read responsibly.

## Upon entering Club Sin, you are consenting to the following:

1. You are STI/STD free.
2. You are healthy and able to engage in or observe sexual activity at Club Sin.
3. You are on or have brought birth control of your choice.
4. You consent to engage in the kink of your choice upon entering the room of your choice. Anyone is welcome in the room that represents their kink with consent; privacy is maintained when requested. Multiple partners are common and encouraged at Club Sin.
5. No kink shaming allowed. People are free to explore and enjoy all their desires in a safe and consensual environment at Club Sin.
6. Honesty and communication are key to a satisfying experience at Club Sin.
7. Discretion and privacy are valued at Club Sin.
8. No cell phones are allowed in Club Sin.
9. Universal safe word at Club Sin is RED, unless otherwise agreed upon. Be aware of non-verbal cues.

## At Club Sin we want you to have a satisfying experience. Go and play!

# CHAPTER ONE

## LUCI

"You know what they do in there, don't you?"

I nod.

Of course I know.

I don't like it. But I need the work, the kind that comes with flexible hours, low stress, and minimal tendency for taxing my brain. My mental energy and remaining waking hours are reserved for my bookkeeping course. I've got my eye on the ball, as they say. There is no wavering. No deviation.

Bookkeeping is my ticket out. My golden egg. A launching pad to a new life. So, my job, regardless of 'what goes on there,' is a means to an end. I need just enough money to cover my day-to-day and tuition at the community college, which isn't a lot for most people. But it's a lot of money for *me*, someone on the cleaning crew of a… whatever the place I work for is called.

I didn't exactly look for this particular job. No, I went to an employment agency I found out about through the college jobs board, and some nice lady there sent me to interview for a cleaning job at a private club.

I had no idea what a private club was. Never been to one. No one in my family is a 'club type.' Whatever that is. So, yeah, I regularly see some crazy stuff here. Stuff that doesn't jive with who I am or where I come from, but that doesn't matter. I'm focused on my goals.

Someday I will have a nice office job where I wear tailored pants and a blouse—made of silk, if I do really well—and sit at a desk and computer, rather than clean cum off sofas, floors, and walls like I currently do.

That'll be the day.

Until that happens, I try not to think about it too much. Which is nearly impossible when silver-haired Sam, the kindly attendant at the cheapest parking lot within a several-block radius of the club, keeps reminding me he thinks the place I work for is dirty and messed-up.

I mean, it is. But I don't think about it.

I lock my car and hand over my five dollars, smiling at Sam for looking out for me. "I know, I know, Sam. I just gotta get my certificate and then I'll be out of there."

He doesn't look convinced, as evidenced by his wrinkled brow. He's taken a liking to me, for some reason, ever since the first day I parked here. I guess I brought it on when I breathlessly told him how happy I was to have found his lot. Parking lots closer to the club are twenty dollars and up—way too rich for the blood of a cleaner like me who's barely making minimum wage. Sure, I have to walk a few more blocks, and when it's late and dark outside, I carry my pepper spray in my right hand, ready to unload it on anyone up to no good. But at least I'm taking home a bit more cash. It all adds up.

I pull my hoodie up and stuff my hands in my pockets. It's broad daylight, so the pepper spray rests in my little crossbody bag, not due to come out until I'm heading home at the end of my shift.

"Alrighty, Luci," Sam calls after me. "Be careful there, won't you?"

I don't have many people in my life looking out for my best interests, and hearing him affirm his concern for me, as he often does, knocks against my chest in a part-happy, part-sad reminder of who I am.

I mean, yeah, I have parents and friends. But they are all puzzled as to why I 'left it all behind' to come to the dirty, dangerous city of Chicago. I don't need a silly bookkeeping career, they tell me. Settle down, marry a nice boy from church, and squeeze out some babies. Heck, that had worked for my mother and her mother. Why do I need anything different?

But what they really want to say, which I can see on their faces and hear in their words, is why do I *deserve* anything different?

I can't answer that. I just know I do.

I look over my shoulder, half-tempted to run back and hug Sam. Thank him for caring about a relative stranger and tell him know how rare he is, and what a gift like this means to someone new to town with few friends, a hellacious job, and who's constantly worried about the lights being shut off, running out of gas, or not being able to find enough ramen noodles to last through the week.

But I don't. I just wave at him with a little laugh, as if I have everything under control. But I can tell by the way he's looking at me, he knows as well as I do, I'm faking it.

Just before I enter the club, my phone rings. I

wouldn't normally answer because I'm a freak about getting to work early. Again, I can't mess up this ride I'm on, and a misstep in any direction could bring it all crashing down on my head. But I see on my crappy little non-smartphone that it's my mother.

"Mom? I'm about to go into work. Can we talk tomorrow?" I ask. I look at my cheap Timex watch and see I have plenty of time before my shift. But I'm not about to mess up my perfect attendance record now, not if I can help it.

The club manager, Gwen, isn't exactly what one might call understanding. Or nice. Or even decent.

"Oh, Lucinda, I wish you would just come home," Mom sighs. I picture our kitchen, slathered in an amazing array of strawberry motif, where Mom is looking around for a possible speck of dirt to clean, tapping her pink fingernails on the pink wall phone.

I think of explaining to her why I'm there, in the big, bad, dangerous, dirty city—her words, not mine—but such explanation is by now, officially, something I'm getting tired of repeating.

But like a glutton for punishment, I half-heartedly try, anyway. "Now, Mom, you know I can't do that—"

But Betty Jo Braxton isn't going to be deterred. She never is. "Lucinda, you know that place is full of sinners. Fornicators, drug pushers, and murderers. That's no place for a sweet girl like you."

Which begs the question—what place *is* there for me? The one my best friend from high school ended up in? Teenaged, pregnant, forced to marry her creepy baby daddy?

No thanks. I don't even need to ask because I know that was exactly the world my mother and everyone else in our church community thinks is ideal *for a nice girl like me.*

"Mom, I gotta go—"

"Sweetheart, if you're going to be a cleaning woman, at least come home and do it here. I am sure Pastor Sandy can give you work down at the church. In fact, he was asking about you just the other day. How about when you come home for the weekend, we have him over for a nice family barbecue?"

Ugh. Sandy Rollins. He'd been a few years ahead of me in school. Always a simpering little tattletale, prone to crying at the smallest slight. But he'd earned some sort of theology degree from a fly-by-night college, which was good enough for the local parish, which then hired him as a 'youth pastor.'

He took the church's pre-teens and teens on camping trips, organized basketball tournaments, and preached the benefits of keeping one's soul clean.

Even while grabbing my ass every chance he could get.

I knew the type. Jerked off to the nastiest porn he could find, then dropped to his knees to ask God for forgiveness. Later, smug in the knowledge that his soul was clean, he'd just go out and do it again.

That's the worst kind of sinner, if you ask me. The hypocrisy is crushing. I mean, I see some crazy stuff in the club, but at least those people aren't pretending to be holy rollers. They might be sinners—who am I to judge?—but they don't spend their days and nights telling young girls to wear longer skirts and boys to keep their hands off their uncontrollable erections.

So a barbecue with that creep? Hell to the no. But I have to tread lightly. "I don't know about that, Mom. You know I'm not a big fan."

She sucks in a sharp breath, her 'godly' way of letting me know she's 'disappointed' in me. "Well. I'll let you get to work now. Have a blessed day, Lucinda," she says curtly.

*Click.*

There was a time when her hanging up in my ear, like she just had, would have caused me no end of anxiety, borne out of the guilt of not being a perfect daughter. But now, it just relieves me. It buys me some time before the next Mom intervention. And yes, there'll be another one. There always is.

I wait across the street from the club to catch my breath before going in, still abundantly early thanks to my obsession with timeliness. As I do, I watch a man enter. I've seen him before, but only from a distance. He moves with such confidence and authority, I wonder exactly who he is. In fact, just looking at him makes me shake even though I'm hiding out in the street corner shadow, hastily disguised with my hair tucked down the back of my hoodie and the drawstring pulled tight around my face. He doesn't see me. None of these people do. But I see them. I watch them. I can't help it.

He's handsome. Of course. It seems like a requirement of the club that members be generally good-looking, although I've seen exceptions to that rule if one has enough money. I don't know how something like that is even legal, but heck, the stuff they do here, if it's not against the law, is surely immoral on some level.

Naturally, Mom has no idea about that part.

Nor does my father, nor the creep Sandy. And they never will. All they know is that I am the cleaning woman for a private club. They have no clue I pick up after people who do all manner of intimate, adult, *sexual* things in the privacy of the club's rooms. And there are a lot of rooms. So many that I am busy from the moment my shift starts to the moment I clock out. Which is just as well. I don't really want to think too hard about what I am doing.

The man disappears into the club, the imposing security door seemingly having sucked him inside. I take my time crossing the street, regardless, in order to let him get where he's going. If my path crosses his, I might be obligated to say hello. I don't want that. I don't want him to see me, acknowledge me, or even know that I am alive. I am part of the behind-the-scenes nobodies who keep the club up to its exquisite standards, which then keeps memberships elusive and expensive. The three E's, as my boss likes to remind me.

I shouldn't want to know his name. I shouldn't want to know where he lives. I shouldn't want to know what he does for a living, nor why he comes to the club.

Except that I do.

I'm curious. Nosy, some might say. It's true.

When I hear the cries, moans, laughter, and screams escaping the club rooms, my heart rate picks up. Sometimes I even get a little breathless. For a moment, I'm not thinking about what I'll have to clean up after the people are done but what they are doing until that time. All those *immoral* things.

And of course, I feel something *down there*.

It's a funny feeling, one I've not experienced much, but the strange pressure that builds, a combination of having to pee and something else I don't have words for, electrifies me. I can't deny it. Once, I even ducked into the storage closet for a moment to myself. I started to slip my hand down my panties, the tidy white cotton ones my mom's been buying me all my life, but I stopped.

I would wait. For what, I wasn't sure. But I'd know when the time was right.

Does that make me as bad as the people at the club?

I hope so.

# CHAPTER TWO

## LUCI

"How's it going, Luci?"

Wow. She must be in a good mood. More often than not, my boss, Gwen, is on the warpath and it's peons like me who have to take her guff. But the times I've seen her slip into one or another of the club rooms for a while with someone for some 'private time,' which I think she's not supposed to, she emerges pretty darn happy. And her good mood lasts all day. Maybe today is one of those days.

Which works for me just fine. I don't need anybody riding me. I keep my head down, do my work, and go back home to study for my course, usually with my friend, Charleigh.

I try to act like the bright smile on her face is a normal thing, rather than throwing me off. "Hello, Gwen. How are you today?" I ask perkily. Unless she asks me a direct question about my work, this is normally the extent of what I say to her.

She's tall and wears extremely high-heeled red-patent leather Mary Janes so I'm always looking up at her. Everyone is. I think she likes it like that. Her hair—I'm not sure if it's a wig or real—is most often a mass of stylized curls gathered at the crown of her head, the rest tumbling down her back. She wears skin-tight corsets, sometimes by themselves and sometimes over blouses with puffy sleeves and ruffled collars. Her skirts often barely cover her behind, but occasionally also hit below her knees.

Another employee, the bartender, tells me her style is called *steampunk*. I've never heard of that before. Sort of old fashioned and modern at the same time seems to be the gist.

Where I'm from, people don't dress like that.

I suppose my personal style is best described as Target. As in the store. Maybe GAP if they're having a good sale. But that's not what I wear when I work as a cleaner. No, I wear a light blue button-up thing they give us maids that looks like one of those dresses nurses used to wear. It's fitted, showing off my figure, but ugly at the same time. Not that I care. And with it, I wear my Converse Chucks, the only name-brand thing I own.

I'm not here for a fashion show. Much as I might enjoy watching and listening, I'm on the sidelines. It doesn't matter how I look, because no one notices me anyway. Which is the way it's supposed to be. I'm a spoke in the invisible wheel that keeps the club running, so people like Gwen can be beautiful, and the man I saw entering earlier today can remain sexy and mysterious.

There. I said it. He's sexy.

Where I'm from, *sexy* doesn't figure into our lives. It doesn't even cross anyone's mind. People are too occupied with being *holy,* as holy as they can be, and whenever possible, holier than everyone else. It's like a contest. A contest I am never going to win.

Gwen looks me up and down, as if to ensure I am sufficiently frumpy, and nods. "Please start with Room 21. The current occupants just finished and we have someone else coming in soon."

"Sounds good, Gwen," I say and grab my tote of cleaning products. And gloves. Lots of gloves.

Gwen likes to warn me about using too many

gloves. About wasting them. They cost money, she says, as if I am stupid enough to believe they grow on trees. So, every shift, I stash as many as I can in the bottom of my tote. I'm not cleaning up anybody's slime without them. I don't care what she says. As if the job wasn't already degrading enough.

I pass several rooms, some with doors open and some with doors closed. Today is quiet. The calm before the storm. Things don't really pick up until after dinnertime. The weekend is when most people come. *All* the rooms are booked then, and there are three or four cleaners like me on duty.

The cleanliness of the club is one of its most important offerings, Gwen always says. Dirt is the first thing to drive people away in a place like this. I would have thought sexually transmitted diseases were the deal breaker, but I guess the condom rule takes care of that. From the number of discarded ones I see in the trashcans, it seems like people are pretty on top of safe sex. They could open a darn sperm bank with all the discarded cum. Just gather up the clear, knotted little balloons full of milky white stuff and get rich.

I reach Room 21 and thankfully, the door is open. Even if Gwen tells me a room has been vacated, should the door is closed when I arrive to clean it, I have a mini panic attack that there just might be someone still in there, doing whatever they do. Walking in on someone is one of my biggest nightmares. It's one thing to clean up after members, but another to see them… going at it.

It's not like I am a prude. I've had some… experiences myself. Not a lot, but enough. There was that one boy at church camp. It was the first time for us both, but we were so scared of pregnancy, not to mention the wrath of God, he pulled back out the moment he was barely inside me. But that counts. At least I think it does.

There was also the time that one guy tried to force me, outside in the parking lot after one of the church socials. I try not to think about that.

I get to work on Room 21 imagining, in spite of myself and my guilty conscience, what had gone on before I arrived to clean. Who had undressed first? Did they take everything off? Did they kiss? Or was it impersonal?

And most importantly, at least to me, is whether the woman enjoyed it as much as the man.

Room 21 is one of the basic rooms, and by basic, I mean it doesn't have any weird stuff in it. Some of the other rooms have swings, thrones, and a weird cross thing. This room has floaty white curtains billowing from the ceiling, white shag carpet, a bed in the middle made up with soft cotton sheets and a real silk coverlet, and a couple overstuffed chairs in the corners.

The club spares no expense, aside from Gwen bugging me to sparingly use disposable gloves. I know all this makes membership expensive—how could it not?—but when I ask how much, Gwen smiles down at me and tells me it's none of my business.

Personally, I do think it's my business, but I keep that to myself.

I pull the linens off the bed and remake it, dumping the used sheets down the hidden laundry chute. I clean all the surfaces, empty the trash, restock the condoms in the nightstand, and generally put the place back together. It is immaculate. Beyond perfect. Like no one had ever been there. As a last step, I mist the room with our signature essential oil room fragrance. I take a good look around.

It's almost like being in heaven, that's how beautiful it is. I'm quite pleased with my work.

According to my Timex, it's a few minutes before the hour, which is when people usually arrive for their rooms. I poke my head out the door to make sure Gwen's nowhere in the vicinity, and re-close it with a soft *click*.

I know I shouldn't do this. But I'm going to. I want to experience the luxury of the club, *just once*. I work so hard to keep it nice. Can't I enjoy it for just a moment?

The smell of the room, a members' room, is the scent of all that is beautiful and perfect in the world, and I imagine for a moment if I could stay there forever, I know I'd be blissfully happy. I float around the bed, fingering the yards of gossamer creating its otherworldly effect, and run my hand over the bedspread.

It's perfection. I have to say am a champion bed-maker. The silk coverlet is taut but not too taut, without a wrinkle in sight. The lucky people who use it next might not notice, but I've been assured—thank you, Gwen—that if it's *not* perfect, that's the first thing anyone sees.

The focal point of every room in the club is where the, um, *fun* takes place, and in this room it's a bed that looks made for a fairy princess.

Against my better judgment and every other bit of rationality I have, I sit down on the edge of the bed, as if I am a woman waiting for someone—

someone who knows how to make me feel sexy, beautiful, and worthy of such lush surroundings. The silk is pure bliss under my fingers, and the bed's firmness indicates it's one of those designer mattresses that costs thousands of dollars.

Which is crazy, because no one ever actually *sleeps* on these beds.

I slowly lower myself down, my head hitting the pillow while keeping my sneakers away from the white silk. I let my eyes fall closed and spread my arms out to take the whole thing in and inhale deeply.

I don't know how much people pay to join, but I am sure it's a lot.

Like more than my rent and school tuition combined, several times over.

And at that moment, Room 21's door flies open.

Oh god oh god oh god.

I'm fucked. Completely and totally fucked.

Sure, there are other cleaning jobs around, but this is the only one that pays slightly over minimum wage and gives me time to study. Am I about to be out on the street?

One little mistake, one lapse in judgement to serve my insatiable curiosity, and it's all over. I've just messed up and will have to move back home. Forget bookkeeping and forget the club.

Bracing myself for a scolding and worse, I bolt upright, but before I can get to my feet, the man entering the room gestures for me to lie back down.

*What?*

And as if that's not bad enough, he just so happens to be the incredibly handsome man I saw arrive earlier, when I was waiting out on the street, hiding like a stalker. It's the man who walks like a real master of the universe, and for whom the waters probably part anytime he requests it.

He is also the sort of man I'm generally invisible to, but not right now. No, he's looking right at me. I am no longer unseen. This is a mistake. A bad one. People like him don't look at people like me.

Disregarding his gesture to stay where I am, I jump to my feet. "Oh my gosh, I'm sorry—"

But he stops me. Not with his words or gestures, but because he's loosening his tie.

He's not even waiting for me to leave the room?

"Gwen told me she'd send me someone very special today. She really delivered," he says with a flash of a smile and dimple that makes my knees knock.

Gwen? Someone special? She delivered? I don't get it.

"I… well, I…"

I want to tell him I'm just the maid but the words aren't coming. It's like he cast a spell over me. Or maybe I'm just an idiot transfixed by a handsome man.

Who maybe thinks I'm someone other than who I really am.

"As always, she's outdone herself," he continues, either ignoring or not noticing my silence. "My name is Max, by the way. Go ahead and relax. You can sit back on the bed. We can start out any way you want, Izzy."

Huh? He thinks I'm *Izzy*?

But I'm *Luci*. Luci Braxton.

Yes. That's what this is. He thinks I am Izzy, the woman he has a date with today, in this room, right now, according to my Timex.

Where the hell is she? And why does he think I'm her? I look at the door. I can make a break for it. Not that he'd try to stop me. It's just that if I don't run, fast, I might change my mind about leaving.

"How'd you like to get started, Izzy? Shall we just dive right in?"

I open my mouth to speak, but I'm so dry I

clamp it shut before I look like a fish gasping for air.

The room, which only minutes ago I imagined was my magic fairyland, is suddenly stifling hot, and I can swear the walls are closing in, getting closer and closer, while the fabric billows like long fingers reaching for my neck.

*Get a grip.*

I think this is what's known as a panic attack.

*Reframe, reframe, reframe,* I chant to myself, something I saw in the psychology magazines I used to sneak-read at the public library, which my parents had told me were full of the work of the devil.

Oh my god.

This man, Max, thinks I'm his date. He is pleased to see me and grateful Gwen sent me to him.

It's all unfolding before me, like clouds parting to show blue sky. I know what's going on here, and I know what I'm going to do. It's wrong. And yet...

There's nothing to be afraid of.

Yeah, right.

*You know what goes on in there, don't you?* Sam's words carp at me.

I do know, or at least I sort of know, if my

cleaning up here at the club has taught me anything.

"Would you like to start, Izzy? Happy to follow your lead," he says.

Wow.

I don't expect him to be so nice. He's a member of Club Sin, and if there's one thing I know from my upbringing, it's that sinners aren't nice. They are bad, bad people. And I've always been warned to stay away from them.

And yet here I am, surrounded. But it's not like anyone's holding a gun to my head. I can walk out anytime I want. I can work somewhere else, the downsides of that notwithstanding.

I can even move back home, go back to church, marry a nice boy, and make my mother happy.

But I haven't. And I won't.

I am here because I want to be here.

I take a deep breath to calm my shaking. "It's nice to meet you, Max," I say in a soft but steady voice, hoping it hides my uncertainty. And trepidation.

I still have no idea why he thinks I'm his date, but I'm going to play along until it blows up in my face. It might be my last day at Club Sin, so I have to make it worth it.

I want to know what happens in these rooms,

not in an abstract sense, but really, literally know. Like *experience* it.

The push and pull of the contradiction I'm facing makes me dizzy. What's going to happen? I don't know, but it can't be worse than my job, cleaning up cum and throwing out used condoms.

Am I about to be a sinner too?

---

# CHAPTER THREE

## MAX

As always, Club Sin delivers.

Gwen might be a little strange with that Victorian-slash-punk clothing she wears, not to mention the crazy wigs, but she rules Club Sin with an iron fist and never disappoints.

God bless her.

When she suggested sending me a maid for a little play-acting, I jumped at the chance. I figured she'd get me some little hottie with one of those cheesy costumes they sell at Halloween time, with the tight top and flouncy skirt barely covering the ass. The kind where the maid wears a cute little hat and carries a feather duster like she's actually

35

going to clean something. Stockings and high heels go without saying.

But she's outdone herself today. I mean, what she's set up for me might not work for some guys. I figure my colleagues Gray and Rowan, also prominent members of the club, would probably not be down with today's offering, but I'm always open to something a little different.

Why the hell not?

I've been carrying around a hellacious set of blue balls for a couple days, building anticipation rather than jacking myself to relief. It will make the eventual release all the sweeter. I do that sometimes. It's agonizing, but it's my thing.

Yeah, I'm fucking weird. But we all have our kinks, right?

It's not lost on Gwen what I am in need of. In fact, she offered herself, as she sometimes does. But I let her down gently, as always, saying it's best not to mix business and pleasure, which we both know is total bullshit. But I can't do her. She's not my type. Not by a long shot.

No, I like them like Izzy, standing here before me, sporting the quintessential girl-next-door look. What man doesn't love that?

Every boy's adolescent fantasies start with some girl in his neighborhood, one he might have grown up with. This little thing, maybe pretty and maybe not, develops into something that sparks his first wet dream, and later his frequent attempts to relieve a never-ending erection. The object of my affection back in the day had been Suzie, or Sandra, or some such, living two houses down, and for my entire fourteenth year, I watched her come and go out of the windows of my house whenever I could. I imagined she was heading right over to take my loathsome, humiliating virginity because we know that when a boy is fourteen, he always thinks he's the only one in his circle of friends who's not yet gotten laid.

Just like jerking off, massive lying is one of the hallmarks of a teenage boy's life.

Standing before me today is a specimen of girl-next-door who puts my teenage crush to shame, notwithstanding the frumpy polyester maid's dress and the sneakers she's wearing, made all the sweeter with the long blonde braid pulled forward off her shoulder like a freaking milkmaid.

Which might be another good idea for a role-play, a scene carrying out some of the kinky shit that haunts my dreams. And, if I'm honest, my waking hours. I'll have to bring this up with Gwen. See if she has any tricks up her sleeve.

Like what's before me right now. This girl is

perfection. She not only looks like a real, live maid, not one out of a costume shop, but she also has the nervous, innocent thing *down*. Like Academy-Award-winning down. Shit, the way she's wringing her hands and is basically too scared to even speak has my engine revving at high speed.

Fuck, I hope she's into anal.

I also hope she's wearing granny panties. I already know I'm gonna come all over them and make her put them back on. I love nothing more than a woman stewing in my cum.

Repugnant, maybe, but I've never claimed to be some sort of nice, normal man. I have good manners when I want to, which fools people into thinking I'm a nice guy.

They never realize I'm not until it's too late.

Suits me well in my line of business.

But this girl, this Izzy, really plays up the fear thing. She's clenching, then extending her fingers like she's about to jump out of her own skin. Her eyes are wide, and if I'm not wrong, she's even trembling a little.

Fucking awesome.

Kicking our scene into gear, I stalk around her, throwing no end of dirty looks. "Now, Izzy, I thought I told you to clean this room," I growl.

I actually prefer that she start, but I don't have all day.

Plus, it's nice to mix it up a bit. The women I usually role play with are always so eager, over-acting to the point where it takes some of the wind out of my sails. I mean, sure, we're playing, but let's mix shit up a bit.

Her mouth opens and closes. Again. God, she's good.

I take a couple steps toward her, and she tries to step back, but the bed's behind her and she falls onto it.

"Um, um… I'm, um… sorry," she sputters.

"Do I need to take you over my knee? Again?"

Something I can only describe as horror washes over her face. She's so believable. So fucking believable.

"N… no, sir. I… I don't want a… spanking," she spits out with a little more resolve.

I clap my hands so loudly she jumps. "Okay, then. There's dust over there," I say, pointing at nothing.

She just looks at me.

"Izzy. What are you going to do about it?"

Understanding washes over her. "Right. Right," she says, running to the little bucket she brought with her cleaning supplies.

I'll be damned. She brought real cleaning supplies. No fake shit for this one.

She bends over to root through her props, and just as I'm getting a sense of her ass, she pops back up with a feather duster.

That's what I'm talking about.

Looking back at me with a little smile, she starts swinging it around, as if she's really using it.

And she starts humming. Seriously. And damned if it doesn't sound like some kind of song you hear in church.

My balls had already been tight but now they're screaming in protest, begging for the relief I'd starved them of for the past few days.

*Calm down, you bastards. You're about to get off.*

I'm going to make this last. At least for the hour or so I've got the room for.

"That's very good, Izzy," I bark, following her movement. "Now, sweetie, while you're working on that, could you just unbutton your dress for me? Not all the way, though. Just enough to see your tits."

She might have been across the room from me, pretending to dust, but I clearly see that she stiffens at my request. Slowly turning, she finally faces me with an expression of combined humility and defiance.

And now, my dick's full-on hard, straining against the trousers belonging to my three-thousand-dollar suit. I reach down to adjust myself, really wanting to just whip it out, but forcing myself to slow down. The session cost me a thousand dollars, after all, and while that's a drop in the bucket with regard to my finances, I didn't get rich by being a spendthrift.

Actually, I got rich 'acquiring' large contracts for building and trucking projects, and other lucrative activities like facilitating the movement of drugs, stolen art, and antiquities. Things like that, which, while incredibly profitable, have made it hard to have a woman in my life. A permanent woman, that is.

Thus, why Club Sin is so important to me.

Izzy's wide-eyed gaze is directed right where I'm stroking myself with my flattened palm, and I widen my stance for more breathing room in my boxers.

Damn if her lips don't open the tiniest amount, followed by the tip of her pink tongue moistening them.

Tucking the dusting tool under her arm, she reaches for her dress buttons, starting at the very top. When she gets to those just between her tits, she arches a little, pulling open the dress, and by god, this lovely little thing is not wearing a bra.

Thatta girl.

"What did I tell you about wearing a bra under your uniform, Izzy? Do you want to be like all those other sluts out there? Not wearing proper undergarments?"

She looks down and shyly unbuttons one more. "N... no. I don't want to be a... slut, sir. But... I... can't afford a bra," she says in a whisper.

I cross my arms hard. "Why didn't you tell me this, Izzy? If you need money, you know I'll give it to you. Now, are you pantyless too? Because you'd better not be."

The swell of her small breasts is just so delightful—thank god she doesn't have fake tits, I am so over them—and when she reaches the buttons at her waistline, I catch my first glimpse of her firm tummy.

This girl is so what I need right now because there, what I am so goddamn desperate for I would actually have paid ten thousand dollars instead of one, before me is a peek at the waistband of her white cotton panties.

Goddamn.

"I do have underpants on, sir. Just like you told

me. I… I don't want to be a slut. Like those other girls," she breathes. "Those sluts."

She says it with just the right amount of disdain.

Oh god, my cock is aching. This girl is beautiful and plays the innocent with skill unlike anything I've ever witnessed. And I've done scenes with a hell of a lot of women, some where I paid, like this one, and some with women who were so good they should have been paid.

It's my thing. What can I say?

"You look very pretty, Izzy," I say, wondering how much longer I would be able to keep my cock in my pants.

She looks down at her sneakers, all blushing shyness.

Goddamn, this girl is gonna be my new favorite.

"Thank you, sir," she says so quietly I can barely hear her.

I approach, and she clasps her hands, her dress opening down the front of her body, exposing a long, narrow slash of skin.

I raise my hands to her shoulders, taking the collar of her dress. She flinches at my touch.

Fuck yeah.

"Now, Izzy, I'm going to slip your dress off, okay. But don't be afraid, I won't hurt you."

She finally looks up at me, and in such close proximity I see her blue eyes contain specks of a still-darker blue, like someone painted them, then scraped away the top layer to expose the color underneath.

I slide the shoulders of her dress—it really is a polyester piece of shit, I'll have to thank Gwen later for that—off her shoulders. It slips down her arms and to the floor, where it puddles on top of her sneakers.

One arm rises in a lame attempt to cover her nipples, now stiffening from the exposure.

I take a step back. "Now, get back to your dusting."

She picks up the feather duster, which had tumbled to the ground at some point, and steps out of the dress circling her feet. Turning her back to me, she waves it at an imaginary piece of furniture, giving me a perfect view of her lovely back, the heart shape of her ass under her loose panties, and her strong thighs.

"Baby, pull your panties between your cheeks for me," I say, unable and unwilling to hide the growing rasp in my voice.

She takes a quick look over her shoulder, as if for reassurance.

I nod. "C'mon, honey. You can do it."

She drops the duster again and slips her fingers under the elastic of her panties, slowly sliding them toward her crack, exposing the smooth, lovely skin of her ass.

She stops when they are halfway exposed.

"More," I growl.

When they are completely wedged between her cheeks—it probably isn't too comfortable, but I don't really care—I walk over and place a hand on her shoulder.

"Bend forward."

She glances back again, then slowly bends, aided by the gentle push I give her, until she's at a ninety-degree angle, her hands on the sitting chair for balance.

"Stay there," I say.

I step back to see the white cotton bunched up, then smooth over her pussy lips, nearly visible through the thin cotton.

"Are you shaved, honey?" I ask.

"N... not really," she murmurs.

I smooth a hand over one of her ass cheeks. "Why? Why not, Izzy?"

"B… because I don't want to be a slut. Like the other girls."

Great answer. This girl is earning herself a big fucking tip.

"Let me see. Pull your panties aside."

She gasps, but without missing a beat, reaches around and gathers the panty fabric—seriously, those fuckers are *huge*—unwedges it from her ass, and pulls the fistful aside to show me her pussy.

I sigh as I find that, as she said, she's not shaved, but that her hair is sparse, being a blonde and all, and that her lips and lovely little slit are easy to see.

I crouch down for a better look, and fuck if she doesn't smell amazing.

"Looks like you're a little wet there, Izzy," I say. "Are you?"

She takes a moment to answer me, her breath coming in shallow rasps. "I… I don't know."

"Touch yourself, Izzy. Find out for me."

Her other hand comes off the chair she's leaning on and reaches back between her legs, hesitating between her thighs.

"What's wrong, honey? You've never touched yourself before?"

"I… um… no. Not really."

But she cups her pussy and drops a middle finger into her cleft like the good girl that she is.

Fuck if I don't nearly cream myself right there. "Honey, I am going to open my pants and take out my penis, okay? I won't touch you with it."

Something about sounding so clinical makes our game feel all the dirtier.

I get to work unbuckling myself, something I've been dying to do since the first moment I laid eyes on her long blonde braid and polyester maid dress. The relief I feel when my cock is finally untethered feels like a million bucks and I sigh loudly.

There is a swell in my balls, but I'm not going to come yet. I fist my cock until it hurts and the head turns purple, showing the goddamn thing who's boss.

Yeah, right.

"You feel the wetness, baby? Is that pussy nice and wet?"

Her body moves, and I see she's nodding her head. "Yes. It's wet," she says so quietly I can barely hear her.

"Okay, honey. I thought so. Now pull your panties down below your ass."

She looks back over her shoulder like she's

done so many times in the last hour, and the sheer terror on her face is unmistakable. And delicious.

But so are her dark dilated pupils, the flushed apples of her cheeks, and the way she bites her plump lower lip.

"Such a pretty girl," I croon, as the white cotton bunches in her fingers and slides to her thighs.

My legs cramp from crouching for so long—goddammit, I thought I was in better shape than this—so I stand, stroking my rigid cock just above her back end, her puckered asshole shuttered tight, leading to the sparse hairs trying to obscure her juicy pussy.

One glance at my watch tells me time is almost up. I really do have shit to do today. Time to wrap up the day's fun.

"Stay just like that," I say between heavy breaths.

Yeah, I planned to come on her pretty ass cheeks.

And in moments, the release my balls had been begging for, and which I denied myself for too long, ruptures in a thick stream of cum, one of the largest loads I've ever unleashed, all over the behind of my pretty little maid.

Interestingly, she neither moves nor makes a sound through my whole climax. I appreciate her playing along until the final moments of our session.

I pull a towel out of the nightstand drawer they are always kept in, wipe my dick and hand off, then throw it onto Izzy's back.

She still hasn't moved from her bent position.

I reach into my money clip and pull out some bills. Tossing them onto her dress on the floor, I leave without a word.

# CHAPTER FOUR

LUCI

THE DOOR to Room 21 closes with a *slam.* But I don't move.

Still bent, I have my hands on the arms of a chair, my behind in the air, and my panties pulled down, showing my... everything.

I also have a thick layer of... ejaculate all over my backside.

The first heave throws me to my knees. I don't want to straighten up because all the sticky stuff on my back will run, so I stay like I am, bent, hunched, submissive. It's not comfortable.

So, I bury my face into the overstuffed chair to muffle any noise I might make while several convulsing waves make their way over and through me, as if trying to teach me a lesson about what I'd just done.

Please don't puke, please don't puke. It will be hard to clean up and will stink, too.

I wait for the tears, which will be easier to manage.

I didn't have sex, but I did do something bad. I just know it. The man didn't really touch me aside from running his hand over my butt cheek, but he sure looked at me. And got me to touch myself.

That was wrong, right? I mean, nice girls in the town I'm from don't do things like that.

But they don't move to Chicago to get their bookkeeping certificates or take cleaning jobs in places like Club Sin, either.

I heave a second time, but nothing comes out, thank goodness. Nor do tears. Am I so dry, so barren, that my body can't even purge my sinfulness? Isn't there a price to pay for the awful, humiliating thing I'd just done?

Letting that man touch me, see me, and smell me is one thing.

But the bigger sin, which I figure has sealed my fate, that of spending eternity in hellish damnation, is... that I enjoyed it.

I *enjoyed* it. That's all there is to it.

I enjoyed his dirty gaze, his filthy words, and the way he spurted his essence on me like I was some sort of trash bin.

The contradictions swirling around my mind are dizzying. But I take deep breaths just like they say to in the psychology magazines—the ones I wasn't supposed to ever read—and in a minute feel calmer.

But I can't sit here like a pile of waywardness for long. Someone will come looking for me, find me with my dress off and panties pulled down, covered in a man's sperm.

Or *cum,* as I've learned to call it.

I grab the towel Max threw my way and strain to reach my back with it. I figure I won't get every last bit of what he let loose on me, but that doesn't matter. What does, is getting back to work before I'm discovered. My Timex tells me I've been in the room for a good hour. Someone will be looking at me.

Like Gwen. And it's never good when Gwen is looking for you.

What did I just do? I heave again, thinking about the self-destructiveness of my actions. There is something wrong with me, something irrevocably, treacherously wrong. I always knew I was different from the people who surrounded me. I never really bought into my parents'—and church's —narrow beliefs about what's right and wrong. I tried to, though, god knew. I prayed and prayed, night after night on my knees on the hard wood floor at the foot of my bed, relishing the discomfort and pain. And yet my doubts never went away. If God wanted me to feel differently, wouldn't he have let me know?

All my friends had accepted the doctrine they'd been fed, hook, line, and sinker. Never was any of it questioned, at least by anyone I knew. Not in my entire life.

So, I kept my own thoughts and questions to myself.

Like, how could it be a sin for a girl to wear a skirt above her knees, tempting boys into 'impure' thoughts?

Why wasn't it a sin for the boys who were tempted with such? And, god forbid, if they acted on those temptations, why was there no fault on their part?

It was still the girl's burden. Always the girl's burden.

It just never made sense.

But I kept that to myself.

When most of the stickiness is wiped from my back, I crawl over to where my dress sits crumpled in a pile, set aside like the ugly thing it is. And yet, somehow it entranced Max. He found something sexy about it and would no doubt have ravished me further had his time not expired.

It isn't the short skirts that bewitches boys. More like the brains between their ears. And the genitals that sit between their legs.

I look at the crumpled innocence of my dress, but there's something about it that keeps me from touching it.

There is money on top of it.

Two crisp one-hundred-dollar bills.

I've never seen a hundred-dollar bill in person.

And now there are two of them right there on the floor, resting on my dress like leaves blown in on a windy day.

They lie there, benign enough as the pieces of paper they are, but dirty and sinful enough to remind me of what I just did.

I didn't know Max was going to leave me money. But now that I have it, it takes no time at all for my thoughts to round the bend from thinking I'm an awful slut to how I can now pay for another bookkeeping course.

Heck, it will cover the textbook too.

Footsteps in the hallway pass Room 21, gratefully yanking me out of my trance. I grab the money and fold it tightly, tucking it into my sneaker, and pull up my dress. I manage the buttons with one hand while I run around the room, straightening it out with the other.

Max and I didn't make much of a mess, thank goodness, at least compared to what I was accustomed to seeing, and in moments everything looks as perfect as it did before he arrived. My fantasy land is restored.

Just when I grab my cleaning tote, the door to Room 21 is flung open.

"What the fuck is going on here?" Gwen barks, flying into the room with Izzy—the *real* Izzy—on her heels.

There was a time when I would wince at Gwen's coarse language. But I've grown used to it. Everyone around me curses, like it's a normal part of speech. People here at the club, people in my bookkeeping course, people in public. It's like I'm the only person on the face of the earth who still says *darn* and *heck*. Well, me and the folks back at home.

"G… Gwen, he just came in. I didn't know what to do," I stammer.

While her hostile eyes bore holes into my soul, I consider other places I might find a job on short notice.

The job board at school has been looking a bit sparse lately, so that's a no-go. Maybe my friend Charleigh knows of something? Her father has a shop, I remember her saying. Although it would be a long drive to get there.

"So, Luci, a top club member comes into the room and you pretend to be Izzy?" Gwen spits.

Izzy looks between the two of us, hands on hips. But her expression doesn't contain the same anger Gwen's does. In fact, she seems to be suppressing a little smirk.

She thinks this is *funny*?

"I... I didn't pretend to be Izzy as much as he assumed I *was* her. He just jumped into things. I went along with it," I say, trying to steady my voice. "I didn't think I should say no."

I didn't *want* to say no.

It's hard to know which is more nerve-wracking—Max mistaking me for Izzy, or Gwen getting mad at me for it.

Of course, she's going to be upset with me. What was I thinking? I had every opportunity to tell him who I really was. And yet, I didn't. My desires—my terrible, sinful desires—got the better of me.

"Hey, Gwen, I gotta head out," Izzy says, winking at me when Gwen isn't looking.

Gwen waves her away, her lips pursed into an angry little line. "Playing out scenes with members is not your job, Luci, in case I need to remind you. What you did was entirely inappropriate—"

"Excuse me, ladies."

My gaze snaps from Gwen's angry face to... Max.

What's he doing back here? Is there an issue? Did he find out I'm an imposter?

Does he have a complaint? And does he want his money back?

I think about the two hundred-dollar bills in my shoe and scrunch my toes, as if that would protect them.

I need that money. I *earned* that money.

What does it matter, anyway? I'm fired, no doubt.

"I came back for my watch, and couldn't help but overhear your conversation," he says.

Gwen's tone does a complete about-face and she is ready to prostrate herself to the man. She does this with all club members. "Mr. Natelli, I cannot tell you how sorry I am—"

But he stops her with a raised hand. "Gwen, Gwen, no need to overreact here. If this lovely young lady here is not Izzy, then I must tell you she did an excellent job in her place."

Gwen's mouth drops open as Max—or Mr. Natelli—crosses the room to the nightstand I saw him place some things in before we got started.

He slides open the drawer, and smiling, retrieves his watch. Snapping it back on his wrist, he turns to my boss.

"I gotta tell you, Gwen, I didn't give this woman here much choice but to play along with me. It's a credit to your hiring skills that even though she might not have been my scheduled girl today, she went with it anyway, making sure I had a good member experience. And her performance was up there with the best of them."

Oh my gosh. He's defending me.

He looks my way and rakes his fingers through his hair to clear the dark, curly strands from his forehead, then flashes me that one-dimple smile he gave me when he first entered the room.

His satisfaction aside, why didn't I speak up when I had the chance? Tell the man I'd go get his date for him?

Why did I have to pretend to be something I wasn't?

Stupid, stupid, stupid.

He heads for the door, but before he leaves, he turns and looks directly at me. "Since I now know you're not Izzy, who are you?"

I think for a moment. "I... I'm Lu," I say.

He doesn't need to know my real name, does he? Everyone else, Gwen included, uses fake names.

"Lu," he says, rolling the two letters off his tongue like they taste good.

*Stop. Just stop.*

"Lu, would you like to meet again?" he asks.

Oh god, no. I couldn't do that. I never should have done what I just did, eating from the wicked apple. But weren't we faced with temptation every day?

And didn't I know better than to cave in to it?

Or did I? Did I choose this place, knowing I'd be tested, surrounded by sinners? That I'd be able to resist, as if I were better than them, somehow?

Did I want to be tempted?

Is that what drew me here?

I nod, almost imperceptibly, as if in doing so, God might not notice. "Y... yes, Mr. Natelli. If that's what you would like, then of course."

He slaps his hand on the doorjamb. "Excellent. And Gwen, I don't think I need to tell you to be sure to treat my girl Lu here as well as you treat the other girls. Am I understood?"

His face is covered in a huge smile, but his eyes carry a warning not even I can miss.

Gwen nods dutifully. "Of course, Mr. Natelli. Anytime you want to meet with… Lu, just let me know." She turns back to face me as he takes off, her expression a modicum kinder. I guess now that she realizes I have some value besides cleaning up cum, I am more deserving of her miserly, reluctant respect.

Such a horrible woman.

With Max gone, Gwen glances around the room to make sure it's in tip-top shape and turns back to me.

"Did you enjoy it?" she asks, her words dripping with annoyance.

Did I enjoy a man taking my dress off, pulling down my panties, and ejaculating on my behind?

I picture the little town I'm from, which molded me into everything I am, and I'm leveled by guilt. What have I done but ruin myself?

But then I think of my life ahead, how there's a whole world out there for me, ripe for the taking, which I can't reach until I unload the baggage weighing me down.

"Yes, Gwen. Yes, I did enjoy it."

# CHAPTER FIVE

LUCI

"This is for you."

Gwen thrusts a handful of cash at me, but I just stare. Like it will bite me. Or at least sully me. As if I hadn't done a good job of that already, all by myself.

From what I can tell, it seems to be more of what Max gave me back in Room 21—one-hundred-dollar bills. But because they're in a folded stack, I'm not certain how much is there.

But I'm looking at multiple bills, of that, I'm sure. Multiple one-*hundred-dollar bills*.

"What is this? What's this for?" I ask.

She rolls her eyes impatiently. "What do you

think it is, Luci? It's your payment. Do you think the girls here meet with members and don't get paid for it?"

I think for a moment. "I don't know. I... never thought about it."

Adjusting the corset her breasts are popping out of, she watches how I look at the money. "Go ahead. Take it. Count it. It's yours. You earned it," she says impatiently, like I'm some sort of idiot.

Maybe I am.

I carefully reach for the crisp bills, as if Gwen might take them back, laughing at me, saying it's all a joke. That a man ejaculated all over my back end, sent me on a death spiral of confusion, and gave me two hundred dollars for it... just for fun, to humiliate someone like me who doesn't know how this sinful world works, even though I sort of want to?

I just want to get back to work cleaning rooms like I am supposed to.

But none of that happens. I accept the money from Gwen, fanning it to find I've been given five bills—five one-hundred-dollar bills.

I now have *seven* one-hundred-dollar bills.

I've never seen this much money in my life. I don't think my parents even have this much money.

I crumple the bills into my fist, just in case someone is indeed planning on taking them back.

"You get fifty percent of what the house gets. Mr. Natelli pays one thousand dollars for an hour of your time, so you get five hundred. And don't gripe about that. I don't want to hear it. You girls always think you deserve more than you do. You have no idea how much it costs to run this place."

Complain? Who would complain about five hundred dollars?

Was she crazy?

Or kidding me again?

"It's… it's great, Gwen. Thank you."

Her face softens when she realizes I'm not going to give her a hard time or ask for more money.

Do the other girls really do that?

Satisfied her breasts are tucked well away, at least for the time being, she continues. "So, good news for you, bad news for me. Izzy, ya know, the person you pretended to be today, is moving on. Leaving the state. Something about a new boyfriend. I'm interviewing for her replacement. Lucky you." She stares at me, her expression bored.

Does the woman have one nice bone in her body?

Actually, I know the answer to that.

She looks me up and down. "You can have her job if you want. We'll have to do a full medical work-up, get you on birth control, that sort of thing. But you'll make a hell of a lot more money working with members than you ever would cleaning up after them. That is, if you *want* to." She clicks her tongue with a huff, her day clearly ruined first by me, and then by Izzy's audacity in moving on.

When I don't answer right away, her face becomes defiant. Like she's daring me to accept her offer. Like she doesn't really want me to accept it, anyway.

"I need to know by tomorrow at noon. If you aren't interested, I need to start looking for someone else," she says, impatient with my silence.

"Can... can you tell me more about the job? Like what it entails and so forth?"

Oh my god. I'm asking for more information when I should tell her flat-out no. A nice girl like me doesn't do *things like that.*

The expectation I'd grown up with, which had been drilled into my head for as long as I could remember—saving myself for marriage—is in my rear-view mirror, getting further in the distance with every passing moment.

She snorts, pressing her lips together. "It's

pretty much what you just did today. The clients pay for 'companionship,'" she says with air quotes.

She rolls her eyes again when she sees the confusion on my face. "Companionship, Luci. That means they pay for your time spent socializing. Doing whatever they want to do. You know, pretending to fuck the maid or whatever Mr. Natelli did with you."

Oh my… does she think I…?

"B… but I didn't—"

She waves her hand. "I don't want to know, Luci. Or should I call you *Lu* now?" she asks with a smirk.

She looks at the clock on the wall. "Let me know by tomorrow. Now, please get back to work, and don't try to steal anyone else's clients."

"I didn't try to steal—"

"Go, Luci," she says, waving me away. "This is a busy night and you need to keep up."

I pull her office door closed behind me, my heart pounding with just how insane the day had already been. I cram the five one-hundred-dollar bills inside my other sneaker and, cleaning tote in hand, head to the next room I need to clean. It's not comfortable, the money stuffed in both my shoes, but I guess that's the point. If I can feel it, I know it's in there.

I like that.

And while the paper in my shoes might not exactly be cushioning, I'm lying if I don't admit it's put a little spring in my step, knowing I've somehow fallen into seven hundred dollars I never planned on having. I don't have to sweat paying for my classes again for a while, which is a relief so massive I want to cry when I think about it.

Maybe I could even get my car radio, stolen on my first night in Chicago, replaced.

But I can't be extravagant. That'll surely lead to questions from Mom and Dad, who know full well what a shoestring budget I'm living on. It's one of the ways they try to get me to come back home, their promises of free room and board, not to mention escape from the dirty, dangerous city.

Yeah, I could live with them for free, but at what cost to my happiness?

The longer I stayed in my hometown, the less likely it was that I'd ever get out. It was like a tree that once its roots are too deep, well, you know it's there forever. It ain't going anywhere.

And that was so not me. No matter what I had to do.

Including sin.

CHARLEIGH LOOKS around the diner where we're having burgers and lowers her voice.

"You did *what?*" she asks, her eyes bugging.

I don't blame her. I'm still in shock myself.

"I… I guess when I took the job there, even though I didn't know *exactly* what went on in the place, I actually kind of *did* know on some level, you know?" I explain.

She nods, her cheeseburger stalled in front of her mouth.

"I mean, what the heck did I think happened in a place called Club Sin?" I try to laugh cavalierly. I am unsuccessful.

She scoots her chair closer, leaning over our table to whisper. "You really pretended to be a naughty maid for some guy you didn't know?"

Darn. I should have kept my mouth shut. She's not going to understand. Heck, I don't even understand.

And yet I did it.

Time to change the subject.

"So, Char, do you think the exam will be tough next week? I mean, we've studied pretty hard. I think we'll ace it, yeah?"

She ignores my question, waving a pointed finger back and forth. "No, no, no, no, no. We're not done with this. And I have to get back to work soon. So, spill."

Uh-oh. I was kind of hoping our lunch date would run out so I wouldn't have to share any more details. What an idiot I was for bringing it up in the first place.

But who else could I tell? Sam from the parking lot?

Charleigh sees the hesitation in my face. "Look, you know I'm not about to judge you. I mean, I might have grown up religious and stuff like you did, but I work in my dad's freaking pawn shop. You know some of the stuff I see go down there. We do business with every freak and his mother. So, your getting it on with some hot stranger is certainly not gonna rattle my cage."

I'm so lucky Charleigh's my friend. We haven't known each other long, only having met recently through our course, but we hit it off from the get-go, and bonded even more strongly when we realized we had similar upbringings. We are the two students in the class who are viciously serious about learning all we can. The teacher sees this in us. She likes it and helps us whenever we ask, calling us 'the bookkeeping sisters.' Charleigh's the first friend I've ever had outside my home 'community' and I want so much to be like her. Sure, she had a similar, repressive upbringing like I did. But she doesn't seem hampered by it.

I giggle, embarrassed. "I wouldn't say I 'got it on' with him," I say, using air quotes.

She impatiently waves her hand. "Whatever. Tell me, did you like it?" she asks hopefully. Like me, she doesn't have much experience in these matters.

*Did I like it?* I've been asking myself that question too, every minute of the day since it happened. I know what the answer is, but I strangely keep expecting it to change. As if I'll suddenly realize the sinful error of my ways and regret the whole thing, admitting just how degrading and humiliating it was. I'll move through being angry with myself, then forgiving myself, then committing to never doing anything like it again.

But that's not actually going to happen because I *did* like it. And no matter how many times I give myself the opportunity to change my perspective, to find the harm in what I did, it stays the same. I don't regret it, I'm not ashamed, and I know I'm going to do it again.

But the confusion, the conflict, won't stop buzzing around my head like an annoying insect.

I raise my eyes to look directly at Charleigh,

whose gaze I was previously avoiding, afraid of the same judgment I've been passing on myself. I nod slowly, terrified to say it out loud.

She slaps her hand on the table, startling me and the others around us. "Okay, then. I had a feeling you liked it. Face it, Luci, you've left behind your old life, and you're forging a new one. Now, I'm not gonna say it will be easy, but you're making it happen." She sits back in her seat, satisfied with her speech. "I'm here for you, girl. And for what it's worth, I think this is hot as all get-out."

Is she a sinner just like me?

The waitress slaps our check on the table and I reach for it before Charleigh can. I have some extra cash now. The least I can do is treat my best friend.

For the first time in my life, I am successful at something, thanks to my course. Not the kind of something where I'm making a cake for the church fundraiser or quilting a square to go in a bigger blanket for someone's baby gift. No, I am really using my brain now. It's liberating, finding that I can do things like understand numbers and what they mean for a business.

Sometimes I imagine I'll even go on to get my accounting degree and after that, become what our teacher calls a *CFO*—chief finance officer, or something like that. She tells us they have a lot of responsibility and make important decisions for a company. I think that sounds pretty cool.

I look around to make sure no one's watching and pull some money out of a hidden pocket I created in the cheap purse I got from Goodwill. I spent a little of my seven hundred dollars, surprised to learn that some places don't like to accept hundred-dollar bills. I guess there are a lot of counterfeiters around, but what did I know? I'd never even held a hundred-dollar bill until twenty-four hours ago. But when I used one at the gas station just that morning, the clerk held it up to the light, looked at me, then turned it over and aimed a little flashlight on it.

That's how they know whether or not it's real.

I carefully slip the hundred out of my purse, and lay it on the lunch bill, careful not to take my fingers off it, as if it might walk off on its own.

"What is *that?*"

I follow Charleigh's gaze as she sets down her empty Diet Coke.

"I'm treating today. I... I have a little extra cash this week and want to do something nice for you."

Her gaze flicks between mine and the money. Like she's not sure what she's looking at.

She sighs. "What I mean, Luci, is where did you get a hundred-dollar bill?"

But before I can say a word, she continues.

"Is that what they paid you? You know, for your... session?" The corner of her mouth hitches up, like she's trying not to smile.

I shrugged. "Yeah."

She just keeps staring, like there's more to the story. Which, of course, there is.

I lower my voice to just above a whisper. "I got paid seven hundred dollars, Char. I was shocked, like you are right now. I just couldn't believe it. I still can't. I have money for my courses now. I don't have to worry, at least for a while."

Her face explodes into a huge grin, and relief washes over me.

"That is so hot," she giggles.

Warmth fills me, an unfamiliar sensation of satisfaction, like when I earned my first A in book-keeping.

It feels good. So good to have some of my worry washed away.

It's funny, what money does. I never knew. It buys this blanket of security. It's a... relief.

But what feels even better is the thrill of what I did to earn it.

And knowing I get to do it again.

# ROOM 21: PLAYTHING FOR THE MAFIA

# CHAPTER SIX

## LUCI

I LIE QUIETLY on the bed, the one I'm usually making up for the next client in Room 21 and try to slow my heart rate. I spread the sides of the lacy white dress Gwen gave me to wear and adjust the white veil over my face. It obstructs my vision but is sheer enough that I should be able to see a little something.

Like when my client arrives.

My eyes dart all over the dim room, the one I know well from cleaning it so many times. Now I'm going to be the one messing it up.

I lift my head from the small pillow to check

my shoes, the white satin Mary Janes Gwen gave me to wear, hoping I'd not scuffed them yet.

Apparently, these costumes are expensive, and Gwen says to keep them as clean as possible.

That's when the door clicks, opening just long enough to allow in a flash of light from the hallway. As soon as it's closed again, the room returns to its candlelit duskiness.

Without moving a muscle, I strain my eyes to look toward the door. I'm supposed to be dead, or asleep, or something—Gwen wasn't really clear— so my eyes are to be shut. But I figure until my client is right in front of me, he can't see me through the veil.

Just like I can barely see him.

But I can see enough to realize it's not Max from the other day, and a little wilt of disappointment waves over me. He was so kind in keeping me out of trouble with Gwen, and so awfully handsome to boot, that I had really hoped he'd come back to see me.

In fact, this past week when I lay awake each night and touched myself *down there*, Max was all I could picture. His dimple and the curly hair he repeatedly pushed off his face filled my imagination with just what I needed to *get off*.

Charleigh's words, not mine.

The bed depresses next to me as my client takes a seat. I open my eyes to slits to see if I can get a look, but with the veil and dim lighting combined, all I can make out is a broad expanse of shoulders and dark hair atop a light-skinned face. He reaches over me, runs a hand down my lace-covered arm, past my hip, and along my leg until he reaches my bare ankle, which he wraps his fingers around. A shiver and a rush of air on my part involuntarily acknowledge this man, and I hear him hum approvingly.

The room is otherwise so quiet that I can hear his breath, steady and slow.

Like he's done this before. Without even seeing him, I know he's full of confidence. Never lets anything get in his way. Has he had an easy life? I'm not sure. But he has success beyond all imagination now, in what I guess are his thirties, and can afford any sort of entertainment he desires.

Including me.

"So beautiful," he whispers, thumbing the bony part of my inner ankle.

My god, his touch feels good, and as his fingers feather up the inside of my calf, without even thinking about it, I part my legs slightly, enough to make sure he continues, but not enough to scream how much I want it.

And I do.

I'm lying if I don't admit I hope this man makes me feel good. Gwen warned me, sometimes the members just want what they want, and that's it. She raised her eyebrows when she said it, looking at me knowingly, to see if I got her meaning.

I did. I was hardly an expert about... intimacy between a man and woman, but I knew from the way she gave me this information not to expect much.

Aside from being paid.

Which, if I'm honest, is *part* of why I'm here. I guess when you have so much uncertainty about... *things*, like I do, it's easier to let someone else take charge. It's like an absolution of some sort. If I'm not initiating it, pursuing it, then I can't be that bad. Right?

The guilt is all on the other person.

Which is completely and utterly ridiculous. I have as much agency as I've ever had. This is all of my own choosing.

"Lu, my lovely Lu," the man chants. He knows my name. He slides the hem of my long dress up to my knees and then my thighs, where he stops.

I want to open my eyes so, so badly. I want to see this man who's marveling over me, this man who's paying money to be with me. A lot of money.

I want to ask him why he does it, and doesn't he have a girlfriend he could do the same thing with at home?

What is it about Club Sin, I want to ask. Why does it have a hold over people like him and me, because I know I'm as drawn to it as Max and this man, whatever his name is, and any of the other beautiful people I pass in the hallways going to and from the rooms we have for them to meet in.

And when his lips fall on mine, right through the veil, I'm able to get part of my question answered, the one about what he looks like. My eyes fly open, and with his mouth resting on mine, I can't see much but I do see his smooth, tanned skin and heavy brow. But the moment he pulls away, I close my eyes again.

I have a role to play.

His hands return to my thighs, where he left the hem of my lacy dress, and he continues sliding the fabric upward, the cool air of the room whispering over my legs, now goosebumped with anticipation. My reaction is not lost on the man, who chuckles quietly.

The white lace thong Gwen bought me, which of course she made sure I knew cost forty dollars, was sheer enough to also let the room's air touch my newly-bare flesh. As instructed, I shaved *down there*, and after the initial shock of seeing myself so exquisitely exposed, the sensation of being bare of pubic hair was startlingly exciting.

Actually, very exciting.

"Pretty, pretty," the man murmurs.

When his lips land on my lace-covered sex, I reveal myself with a gasp. I don't mean to. I am not supposed to. I was to hold perfectly still and not make a sound.

Have I ruined it?

But the man just chuckles again, then presses his tongue into me, or at least as far as the lace barricade will let him.

And in spite of it, the warm wetness of his snaking tongue is pure heaven, a thousand times better than I imagined it would be.

I want to throw my legs open and pull this man's head into me. I want him to taste me from one end to the other, to smell me and feel me and tell me I'm beautiful.

But I can do none of that.

It's not what he's paying for.

My dress is raised clear up to my waist, where it will go no further unless its zipper is opened. But that seems not to bother the man, as he runs his lips across my stomach, laying small kisses on me like searing lashes of sin.

I ball my fists to absorb some of my temptation, hoping he doesn't notice, or at least if he does, he isn't bothered by it.

In a startling movement, the man slides my panties down to my thighs, baring me in a way I've never been seen. Even when I was with that boy at church camp, it was dark. I was too modest to let him see anything, anyway.

The man reaches under my behind and props me up, raising my sex, and next thing I know, even though my legs are tightly bound together by the panty around my thighs, he swipes his tongue through my slit, parting it and opening me to a new world, one I think I will never be able to leave.

And oh my god, it's wonderful. I thought his attentions on the outside of my panties were incredible, but his tongue on my bare flesh is heavenly. My breath is coming hard, and while I'm trying to remain silent, there is just no hiding my reaction.

With his face buried in my sex, I lift my head the slightest bit and gaze down, hoping I won't be caught. He is moving his head only a small amount, just enough to let his tongue reach as far as it can between my lips, constrained as I am by my bound thighs. In his hands are fistfuls of my lace dress, and he is groaning quietly.

He zeroes in on my bud, the one I focus on when I am in bed at night. Placing his lips around my clit, he creates a suction that has me arching up off the bed, throwing my head back, and emitting a cry I've never heard myself make.

I don't care what role I'm supposed to be playing, but I'm neither dead nor asleep and if the man doesn't like it, well, that's too bad. There's no pretending he isn't tormenting me, and there's no stopping my reaction to him. The tickle starts with his tongue and from there ignites like a flame in gasoline, reaching the ends of my fingers and toes in seconds, exploding out of my every pore.

"That's it, Lu, c'mon, baby," he says over my cries.

If he wasn't tantalizing me for so long, I might have been able to control myself, but there's no turning back now. I am coming.

And coming. And coming.

I want *him* and I want *more*. Is that so bad? Would God have made this feel so good if he didn't want us to do it? I hold my breath and wait for an answer, but the only one that comes is another orgasm, merciless and wild.

He slowly winds down, following my lead, and

as he does, he pulls my panties back up and my dress back down to my ankles.

I'm still panting a little, not at all sure what he's going to do next, or what I'm supposed to do, but it's too hard to care at the moment.

I needn't have worried anyway.

He slowly lifts the veil from my face, peeling it off and placing it on the bed. I open my eyes to see him because at this point, I don't care anymore, I have to see the man who made me feel like he did.

And he's beautiful. Intense, narrow eyes, a long straight nose, and thin lips forming the slightest smile all take my breath away. His hair is mussed, sticking up in a few places, and I so want to run my fingers through it to straighten it out.

I don't.

I'm still learning the ins and outs of my work here at Club Sin, and can afford to take no chances. I don't want to lose my ticket to a better life, and I especially want to make sure that if I'm going to be a sinner, I am a damn good one.

# CHAPTER SEVEN

## LUCI

"HELLO, LUCINDA? THIS IS YOUR MOTHER."

While I have a cheap flip phone, it does display the name of my callers, as long as I have them entered into my contacts.

"Hi, Mom. I know it's you, ya know."

She laughs in a polite, obligatory sort of way. "Oh right, honey. I keep forgetting that."

I steer my piece of crap car away from the coffee shop where Charleigh and I were studying, a place equidistant from each of our homes, about forty-five minutes in each direction. I wish we lived closer. But our solution, when we study together, is to split the distance.

"How are things… *there*, Lucinda?" Mom asks.

She still won't even say it.

"Mom, it's called Chicago. It's a major US city. It won't hurt you to say it."

Whoa. That's a little saltier than I usually am with her. I brace myself for a scolding. I might be an adult, but I still get the occasional telling off from her. But she just sighs, no doubt saving her wherewithal for something to come.

I wait for it.

"I was just calling to say hello, Lucinda…" Mom says, babbling on about local gossip like who wore what to church, and how the divorced woman down the street seems to have a lot of gentleman callers.

But my ears perk at one particular name. And not in a good way.

Sandy Rollins. The one man on planet Earth my mother would sell her soul to see me marry.

"… anyway, you two will have a great time, I know it."

"What, Mom? Could you repeat that? The reception isn't great here," I lie. "I'll have a good time with what?"

She sighs. "I was saying, Lucinda, that Pastor Sandy is heading… there, to *Chicago,* for a conference. A youth pastor thing. I told him you'd love to show him around. You know, he doesn't really know the city, and I certainly don't want him wandering alone. I reminded him what a dirty, dangerous place it is," she adds.

I'll bet she told him. Nothing like acting the expert on a place she's never been.

"Mom, I am super busy with school and work. I can't promise I'll be available."

But what I *can* promise, with almost a hundred percent certainty, is that I *will* be busy whenever it is that Sandy comes to town. I don't care if he's flown in from halfway around the world.

There's no way I'm spending time with a man who professes to be holy, but has spent more time staring at my breasts and groping my behind than looking me in the eye.

"Well, he has your number. I might even have given him your address. I can't remember," she says breezily. "He's been under such pressure. You know, he's next in line to be pastor of the whole congregation. He's taking on more and more responsibility. Poor man has been dealing with the church's broken plumbing and everything else."

I steer my car toward the exit that takes me to the club. As always, I'm ahead of schedule. If I have enough time, I can do a little studying in the staff locker room. That is, if Gwen doesn't decide to talk my ear off. As soon as she figured out she could make money off me, she became a lot nicer. Friendlier. More interested. Like she's protecting her investment.

"Mom, how much is it to fix the plumbing?"

Given my recent windfall of cash, I'm feeling generous. I can see it now—my parents will proudly brag that their daughter, one Lucinda Braxton, made a generous donation to the church, thanks to her successful career in Chicago.

*Successful career,* my behind.

And besides, isn't vanity one of the seven deadly sins?

She pauses, then yells something at my father, which I cannot make out because her hand is over the receiver.

A moment later, she's back. "I just checked with your father since he's on the building committee. It's a couple hundred dollars to fix the plumbing, which is not horrible, but it's not the best time for something like this to break. They just put a new floor in the gym and well, you know, we never have much in the way of reserves."

"I'll pay for it."

Silence.

I have no doubt Mom is digesting what I so casually just threw out there, like I'm some sort of high roller or something. And while she is, I'm wishing I could reach out, grab those stupid words, and shove them back down my throat.

Not that I don't want to share what I have, what I look at as recent good fortune, to have work that not only pays more than minimum wage, but that pays at least twenty times more than that.

No, the problem is that my impulsive offer is now going to raise questions. Questions I'm not ready to answer.

With responses that will undoubtedly be lies.

All I can think to do is get off the phone. Fast.

"Where... where did you get money? Extra money?" Mom asks in a slow, suspicious voice.

Can't blame her.

"I... got a raise at work, Mom. I was... promoted." I laugh as cheerfully as I can. "I'm not rich by any means, but it would feel nice to help out. You know, share some of my good fortune."

My mother can suspect the worst of people, which is ironic for a woman who considers herself godly. But what I was learning was that some—maybe not all—of the people I'd grown up alongside were occasionally in the habit of leaping to conclusions about people without reason to do so, and then making ill-informed decisions about them.

So much for giving people the benefit of the doubt. Seeing the best in them. Like I always heard in church every Sunday.

As her daughter, I thought I might be excused. Perhaps not.

Her voice returns after the initial shock that her daughter might have two hundred dollars that she doesn't have. "W... well, that's very nice, honey. How much money do you have to send?"

Ugh. Would that I'd kept my big mouth shut.

"I... I will send a check for two hundred dollars. If that doesn't cover it, at least it will be a good start. Okay?"

I pull into my regular parking lot, whizzing past Sam giving someone directions. He barely notices me, and I am glad. I feel like all he has to do is look my way today, and he'll know what a horrible daughter and big liar I am.

And that he'll know what I did... at the club.

"Hey, Mom, just arrived at work. I gotta run. Love you," I chirp and flip my phone shut.

What have I gotten myself into?

And why am I asking myself that so often lately?

"I've heard a lot about you, Lu."

Rowan Alexo has joined me in Room 21. Gwen told me his friend Max, and the man I saw when I was wearing the lacy white dress, Greyson Orsini —I finally learned his name— really enjoyed their time with me, and so recommended me to Rowan.

She says they're friends and business associates and have been members of the club for a while.

"What do they do for work?" I ask.

Gwen smirks. Always looking for an opportunity to make me feel like an idiot. "Don't worry about that, Luci. There are things you don't need to know."

I lift my chin. "Well, I'd like to know."

She sighs dramatically, then shrugs. "Whatever. They have a few businesses. Syndicates."

Oh. I figured they were doctors or lawyers, the only jobs I know where people make a lot of money. I have no idea what *syndicate businesses* are. But it doesn't seem the time to ask, and to give Gwen another opportunity to point out how she knows everything and how I'm a stupid little minion, even if I am making her a bunch of money.

So, I just smile and slip into my costume.

I have to admit, the dressing up business is fun. Like really fun. I haven't done much… sexually yet, but I think that's coming. Actually, I am sure it is, and the suspense is petrifying and exhilarating. I'm on the brink of something. I'm not sure what, but I am becoming a different person.

Maybe that's why I came to Chicago to begin with. That I knew something was out there, waiting for me.

My heart thumps against my chest when I think about it. I'm not sure whether it's excitement, or rather something trying to tell me what I'm doing is wrong, and that there is still time to turn back.

But there's not. I think it's too late, that is. At some point, without even realizing it, I passed the point of no return. Things in motion tend to stay in motion, and all that.

I am becoming what my parents would call a *bad girl.*

A girl destined for the fires of hell, where I'll rot alone and in pain for all eternity.

It's funny, the things religion teaches to keep people in line. I never really bought it, though. That's how I knew I was different. I sat in church and everyone else would sway with prayer, their eyes closed, experiencing the ecstasy of faith.

Me? I looked around and wondered why God wasn't talking to me. Why was I forsaken when everyone else was so clearly blessed?

Or were they?

"It's nice to meet you, Mr. Alexo," I say, coyly looking up at him from under the thick false eyelashes that took me an hour to apply. That I'd gotten them on at all is thanks to a YouTube video by some beauty blogger.

I bounce a little in my patent leather high heels, clasping my hands behind my back to not only come off as bashful but also push my chest out a bit. I am getting the hang of this.

Rowan's brow wrinkles and he looks unhappy. Very unhappy. And mean. And scary.

He circles around me to get a look from every angle, and my heart pounds against my chest. I knew it might be like this. But I am still anxious. Nervous. Shaky, even.

"It's not *Mr.* Alexo, Lu, it's *Headmaster* Alexo," he growls.

And here we go.

I hang my head. "S… sorry, sir. I won't do that again."

"What else will you not do again, Lu?" he asks, standing behind me, close enough to breathe warm on the back of my neck, but far enough that he wasn't touching me. Yet.

"I… I won't cheat anymore, Headmaster," I say sorrowfully, squirming in my too-tight blouse. "I won't cheat on tests, or copy anyone else's homework."

Naughty school girl. That's what Rowan Alexo wants, and that's what he's getting. Personally, I'm thrilled and think I look kind of cute in my short, pleated skirt, knee socks, and pigtails.

Complete with big red bows.

I actually *feel* myself being scolded because, after all, I really am bad, doing things I should not be, things that are sinful and horrible. Nasty. Degrading. Whorish.

When it comes down to it, this is not truly an act.

"What else will you not do again, you wicked girl?"

I click my tongue like the naughty thing I am. "Well, I guess I won't kiss any more boys. If you don't want me to." I stomp my foot a little and huff.

Rowan circles one more time, just like a predator, only stopping when he's face-to-face with me again. "That's right, Lu. No more boys."

Even with the heels I'm wearing, the highest I've ever worn, I have to look up at him. Not that I mind. There's something powerful about a man looming over me, glaring down at me, menacing me.

Something thrilling in the fear. And the newness of it.

We might be pretending, but at this moment, it feels anything but fake. And with Rowan so close I can smell him and the clean, simple soap he uses, I have to dig my nails into my palms to control my shaking.

"Do you know what happens to naughty girls, Lu?" he asks, running a finger from the notch in my throat down my chest, until it reaches the swell of one of my breasts, hiked up with a very expensive *balconette* bra.

I shiver, watching him trace my inner crease. He lets his hand wander under it until he cups me on the outside of my blouse, massaging me almost to the point of pain.

"I... I don't know, Headmaster. But I don't know that I can stop," I whisper, my gaze locked on his entitled touch. "I know I promised, but the truth is, I don't know if I can keep my promise."

"If that's the case then, naughty girl, I'm going to do something to you before any of those boys do."

There is a tensing in my core, which instantly

spreads, reaching across the flesh of my stomach northward, leaving my nipples hard, pointed, and aching.

"What's that, Headmaster?" I ask in a croaking voice. The shame, the shame of being bad is wafting over me. This might be a roleplay, a scene, to Rowan. But it's not to me. The shame of what I've done and am about to do is palpable. I can taste it, smell it, feel it crawling over my skin.

"I will be taking your virginity, young lady. I want it and will take it before anyone else does." He bends, his free hand reaching behind me, sliding under the pleats of my skirt and resting on my butt cheek.

Little does he know...

I look away, afraid of what I might say with my expression.

He has no idea. There's no way he could.

And he won't find out from me, that I am finally, thankfully, losing my virginity. I mean, really losing it. None of that awkward, lecherous, kid stuff. And while I will pretend to be losing it for this roleplay, it is about the least pretend thing I've done in my life.

# CHAPTER EIGHT

## ROWAN

SOMETIMES I HATE MYSELF.

Actually, it's not just sometimes. It's often. Maybe even a lot.

Like right now.

I have a beautiful young girl trembling at my fingertips. A naughty school girl, I call her. She's about to be punished and then fucked, hard. The way you never would fuck someone you liked, unless you were a total idiot or a sadist. But since this is my fantasy, I get to call the shots.

I want an innocent schoolgirl today. Tomorrow I may want a whore. But that's tomorrow.

And I will fuck her until she begs for mercy,

past the point of fearlessly accepting her punishment. I will fuck her until she cries out, begging me to stop battering her raw pussy.

Why?

Because I am fucked. Fucked up beyond redemption. I have an instinct to humiliate and hurt. I have for years.

But I wasn't born that way.

No, I learned it the hard way, at the hands of my father's enemy.

First, they made me beg for his life. Then they made *him* beg. On his hands and knees, with tears and snot running down his face. Me screaming for them to let him go. Take me instead, I pleaded. My family could survive without me. Just not without my dad.

But they took him from us anyway by shooting him in the head. Right in front of me, so close, the warm, metallic blood splattered, then dripped off my face. Seems like it was yesterday. The humiliation of my begging, the shame of my tears, and their satisfaction in not only taking a man's life but ruining the lives of the people he loved, set me on a path for self-loathing, leaving me with a need to humiliate, as if it would cleanse my soul of the identical stain on it.

And even though I tried to exorcise that stain, it

just never faded. But that didn't stop me from trying.

Like today.

I caress Lu's ass cheek where she stands in front of me, at my direction, of course. It's on the small side for my taste, her bottom, but it's still nicely round, round enough for a girl on the thin side, and firm, as if she is a runner, or at least does a lot of walking.

I slide my fingers into the elastic leg of her panties until my fingers fall between her butt crack. With a forceful motion, I pull one half of her ass open, leaving her to fall into me with a gasp. I take my other hand off her tit and hold her chin, pulling it up to my face, so close I can see the strange specks in her blue eyes, the ones Max told me about.

He sees shit like that. If he'd never mentioned them, I'd never have noticed.

Her lips part the tiniest bit as her gaze locks on mine.

She either *is* a virgin, or a really fucking good actress.

I'm sure it's the latter.

I lean toward her as if to plant a kiss, and as I near her lips, her eyes flutter closed. She is waiting for me. But at the last minute, I bypass her mouth and instead press to her ear.

"Go stand over there," I say, releasing my grip on her. "Over there by the bed."

Her eyes fly open in surprise. She's thrown off. I love that shit.

She stumbles back, surprised by my rejection.

This girl is good. Very good.

Straightening her back, she smooths her skirt where I grabbed her ass, backing up just until she hits the bed.

"Stop fidgeting."

She drops her hands to her sides, her fingers in small fists.

"Don't look at me."

Her gaze shoots to the floor.

I could swear her bottom lip is quivering. This makes my semi-hard dick harder. But I'm not all the way erect yet. That will come.

Now that she's several feet away and I can see her in her entirety, I find she really is as lovely as Max and Greyson swore she is. Normally, I never take their recommendations. They're not nearly as selective as I am.

She's lithe, and in her short plaid skirt and knee socks, coupled with some really high fuck-me shoes, she's quite the fetching number.

I'll have to thank the guys later.

The pleated skirt flares over her hips, accentuating a small waist, which opens up to a nice, round pair of small-ish tits. At least she doesn't have to worry about them sagging when she gets older.

But it's her face that really stops me. Her skin is so smooth and fair it glows and her pink, glossy lips form a perfect little bow. Her long blonde hair is gathered into the perfect pigtailed interpretation of a school girl. All in all, I'm pretty fucking pleased with what Gwen set up for me. She's earned herself a nice tip.

Now, let's see if my naughty girl Lu can do the same. She might be pretty but carrying out a good role play is not at all a foregone conclusion.

"Turn around and put your hands on the bed."

She bites her lower lip and turns quickly, her movements not at all graceful, successfully continuing with her nervousness act. Bending from the waist so she's at a ninety-degree angle causes her little skirt to rise just enough to reveal the lace-trimmed panty I fingered earlier, which is, of course, the plan.

"Head down," I demand.

She complies, and her ass juts further up in the air. Again, part of my warped plan.

And through the crotch of her panties, I see the slight outline of bare pussy lips, and if I'm not mistaken, a little wet spot.

Fuck yeah.

I walk to her, hiking her skirt to her waist, running my hand down her ass to crudely slide it between her legs. I press with two fingers where I know her clit is hiding and while a groan escapes her lips, her little nub escapes its hood. I press harder, applying a general pressure, and she shifts her hips almost imperceptibly to lean into my hand. Like a little beggar asking for more.

Begging is good. Begging is hot.

Begging makes me hard.

"You like this, don't you, Lu?" I ask, intensifying my strokes. "This is why you are naughty, because you like hands on you like this, hands that take what they want with no regard. But it doesn't matter how good it feels. You mustn't do it. You mustn't be so slutty. Now, are you going to keep letting boys touch you like this?" I growl.

She shakes her head, pigtails flopping, her ass waving hungrily in the air. Oh, the contradiction. It's so fucking sweet. This is what I'm here for and this sweet baby is giving it to me like the nice little bitch that she is.

"N... no, Headmaster. I promise," she stammers.

God, I want to take her. Hard and fast, and without her fucking permission.

So, in a swift movement, I bend and reach my left arm under her waist to hold her immobile. I smooth my right hand over her ass cheeks, then pull her panties just below them, revealing a tight little rosebud asshole and pussy lips puffier and more engorged than I'd even hoped they'd be.

And I fucking love thick pussy lips.

"You know what I'm going to do with you, Lu?"

A shiver blasts through her, and I watch her ass cheeks light up with goosebumps. I chuckle. I'm a dick that way.

"No. I mean yes. I mean, I don't know. Headmaster," she says, her breath coming sharp.

"First, you will be punished, and then you will be fucked. That's how I take care of bad girls like you. Slutty girls like you. It's the only lesson you seem to understand. My open palm on your ass and my cock inside you… whatever hole I decide to put it."

She gasps again, and I watch a bubble of juice seep from between her bare lips. This is the kind of response I pay a lot of fucking money for, and this girl has got her act *down*.

"Y… you won't hurt me, will you?" she stammers.

That makes me laugh. "I will, Lu. But then I'll make you feel very good."

And with that, I power my hand down on her bare ass cheek with a firm *slap*.

She jumps, so I hold tighter to restrict her movement.

Another *slap*, and she goes through a litany of sounds, first gasping, because that's always what they do in the beginning, followed by a squeak like someone stepped on a child's plushy toy, and then a groan, as if all that will bleed off the pain.

It never does. But it sounds so sweet.

I lay another three on her, for a total of five before I run my hand over her seared flesh, listening to her breath come hard, like she just ran up a flight of stairs.

"Do you want more, Lu?"

Her head swivels as I touch her pussy, all while calming the skin of her bright red ass.

"No. I mean, yes. Please."

Holy fuck. She wants more. And now my cock is so hard it might just burst out of my bespoke trousers.

I might have to marry this woman.

So, I shift my hold on her to move to her other cheek. No sense in having only half her ass burning with pain, although, from experience, I know this punishment is one of the milder ones I can give. Perhaps next time, when I know her a bit better, I will give her something that keeps her from sitting for a day or two.

Nothing too crazy, though.

I lay my last strike on her other butt cheek, rapidly becoming just as red as the one next to it, and by the time I'm finished, she's panting from the pain, stress, and uncomfortable position. Her legs shake, and I know her balance is off, especially in those high heels.

Fucking perfect.

"How'd you like that, naughty girl?" I ask, performing the obligatory after-spanking rub down.

I am a dick, but not that big of a dick.

Speaking of, I am so hard both my cock and balls are starting to scream in pain.

"Slide your panties off and get up on the bed. Hands and knees. Ass up, chest down."

She looks over her shoulder while I remove my white dress shirt, then kick off my shoes, pants, and boxers. I don't really care whether I fuck naked or dressed, but I have a long day ahead and don't need to be getting cum or pussy juice on my clothes.

Once Lu is up on the bed, I put a hand on each

of her cherry-red ass cheeks, causing her to jump, and bury my face in her cleft. I fucking love that musky, sweaty odor, and even though she clenches as if she doesn't want me back there, she doesn't dare move away.

She knows better.

And, maybe even likes it a bit.

Not that I care.

I drift down to her pussy lips and flick my tongue between them, finding she tastes goddamn delicious. I venture along the length of her gash, straining for her clit, then back to her opening. I pull back and gently pry her open with my thumbs, and what I find is so beautiful I nearly spurt my load right there on the floor.

Her pussy is shaking, glossy and pink, and hungry for attention, and when I return my tongue to it, burying myself in her welcoming cunt, she whimpers.

Fuck me. I need to either get my dick in this woman, or stroke myself, because the throbbing and straining and full-on pain of my engorged genitals will not be bearable much longer. I reach into the nightstand next to the bed and pull out a condom. Sheathing myself, I get to my feet, and pull Lu's ass to the height of my waist.

"Are you ready for your fucking, you bad little

girl?" I ask, sinking one and then two fingers into her pussy to open her slightly.

Maybe I'll do her ass next time. Because there will definitely be a next time.

She jumps at my violation, maybe because it's unexpected and maybe because it feels good. I am not sure.

"Lu?" I ask.

"Y… yes, Headmaster. I'm ready for my… *fucking*," she says, whispering the word fuck as if it's the first time she's ever uttered it.

"All right, baby. Because my dick is hard and I need to be in your pussy, like I need it right now, and here we go…"

I pop my cockhead inside and even though I want to bury myself in one furious stroke, I don't want to come in five seconds. I pulse there for a moment, rocking my hips until Lu takes my lead and pulses right back with the same slow rhythm. My balls are delightfully but painfully making it known that they plan to do what the fuck they want without waiting much longer.

"Do you like it, naughty girl?" I tease. "Do you like the tip of my cock in your juicy cunt?"

Her breath is coming harder and she's gasping now, raising her ass higher in the air, even though I'm barely inside her, but her reaction answers my question. She responds anyway, because that's her job. "Yes, Headmaster. But your… *cock* is so big."

Again, she utters cock like it's a dirty word.

Reaching under, I massage her clit as I slowly push deeper. Fuck if she isn't tight, and when I am buried to the hilt, I hold myself there to enjoy the pulsing of her inner walls, a sure sign her orgasm is forthcoming.

"Oh god," she whimpers, crying a little, holding fistfuls of the bed linens beneath us.

I pause myself there because, yes, I know, I've got a big dick. I wait until her head starts to buck, and for her to grind back against me like a rutting animal in heat, begging for her fuck, begging for release.

And after a minute, her clenched hands pound on the bed beneath us and she struggles for air, her sounds alternating between a high-pitched whine and dirty, raw grunts.

I normally just blow my wad when I'm ready, but for a change, I want this pretty little thing to go before me. She's so delicious and curious in her pretend innocence that I want to see, hear, and feel her come.

And when she does, she shudders so hard she almost comes off my cock, I grab her hips and bury myself like I could actually reach deeper inside her, like reach some sort of holy grail waiting there, just for me, and my perverted tastes.

I love this, I love fucking a naughty little girl, embarrassing her and humiliating her with my dirty words and touch. Max says I get off on this because of the humiliation I experienced on behalf of my father. I hate it when he pulls his psychologist shit on me.

I like this and that's all there is to it.

I squeeze my eyes shut and grimace as my entire groin tenses from the pressure, oh the building pressure, like a balloon filled with too much air that's just on the brink of splitting. I start to shake and the feeling in my arms and legs disappears. All thought abandons my brain and for a few moments in time the only thing in the world is my cock, which is so overflowing with sensation I think for a moment I might die. I am in control, and yet helpless as a madman, and Lu shifts her hips slightly and a vise-like grip flows from my balls to my cock and my explosion begins.

My shoulders shudder as I watch myself pump her. She is tight, so goddamn tight, almost as if I were in her ass, which I will also do. Another day.

I pull out, wanting to get a look at her freshly fucked cunt before I clean up and dress. But when

I go to pull my condom off, there is a little problem.

"What the fuck. Are you getting your period, Lu?"

There isn't a lot of blood on the end of my condom, but regardless, I'm not a fuck-during-the-period kind of guy. I know some men are, and some even seek it out, but I prefer to keep the crimson off my dick, whether I have a condom on or not.

"Lu?" I ask again when she doesn't respond.

Now free from my impaling, she gets to her feet, her panties still pulled down like a dirty slut. She reaches for a towel in the nightstand. "No... my period ended last week," she says, not looking at me.

"Then...?"

No answer.

Oh god, no. No, no, no.

I turn her to look at me, putting my hands on her shoulders. "Tell me, Lu. Was this... your first time?"

She focuses on the tattoo on my right shoulder as if that is where my eyes are, and her lips quiver. She presses them together, trying to control herself, and finally looks back up at me, her face full of shame.

And gives me a little nod.

Godfuckingdammit. If I wanted to fuck a virgin, I'd do it outside the club.

Gwen was going to hear about this.

Lu quietly clears her throat. "I liked it. I really did. Rowan."

This guts me. I don't want to be remembered as anyone's first.

She looks away again.

"For fuck's sake, Lu. What in god's name are you doing working in a place like this, being a fucking virgin? You don't want your first time to be with someone like me."

Her gaze snaps back to mine. "Why?"

I storm around the room, pulling my clothes back on. "Because I'm a fucking asshole. I'm not the kind of guy you want to remember giving your cherry to. I'm a bastard. You... deserve better for a first time."

I can't believe I am saying this. But I mean it. I don't want some girl losing her virginity to me.

What a waste.

———

113

# CHAPTER NINE

## LUCI

I LIMP out of Room 21, not sure where to go next. I know Gwen is waiting in her office, expecting a debrief, and I don't feel like talking about what happened just yet. Not that I'd share all the details with her, anyway. I need some time to think, to absorb what I just did and decide whether it was right or wrong. Was I a slut, or a normal woman learning to enjoy sex? I have no roadmap for this journey I'm on, and at the moment am terribly lost and confused, with a hundred different feelings swirling through and around me, like some kind of crazy storm clouds.

But one thing I am sure of, is that if she learns I

just lost my virginity pretending to be a virgin who wasn't really expected to be a virgin, well, she'd probably give me an earful or even worse, toss me out on my ass. It's not like being a virgin is all that bad, it's just that Gwen doesn't like surprises. She takes them personally, living in a perpetual state of paranoia. How not telling her I'm a virgin could be construed as getting one over on her is beyond me, but I wouldn't put it past her to see it that way.

So, I head for the locker room, which will hopefully be on the quiet side this time of day, without too many of the girls coming in and out, giggling and gossiping, and slamming their locker doors so hard it makes my brain rattle.

I'm heading for the door that says 'staff only,' when I pass a man in the hallway whom I've seen once or twice before. Though not handsome with his puffy face and stumpy build, he looks nice enough, like someone who might coach a kids' softball team on the weekend when he's off work from his office job.

I straighten up and hide the limp caused by the fire on my butt cheeks and the ache between my legs and force a cordial smile. We are instructed to make the members feel important every chance we get, and while I'm in no state of mind to do any more entertaining, I am as polite as I need to be.

"Well," he booms. "Girls didn't look this cute when I was in school," he laughs, stepping in front of me so I can't continue.

Ugh.

But I laugh along with him.

"What room do you work in, lovely lady?" he asks.

I dig up a little energy from the very bottom of my reserves. "Room 21. Maybe you can come see me there sometime," I say with fake enthusiasm. I take a step to get around him, but he jumps to block me again.

Fear surges up my spine, but I know that's silly. I am safe here. There is security. This man can't do anything to me.

He's just flirting.

Being friendly.

"You know, I would like to visit you in Room 21. Why don't we go there right now?" he asks, wrapping his fingers around one of my wrists.

Tightly.

Like, very tightly. Until it hurts.

"Mr..." I say, hoping he'll fill in the blank for me.

He drops his head back with another laugh. "Mr. Doe will be just fine, little lady. Or John, if you like."

He reaches under my skirt, grabbing a fistful of my behind. Such an action would normally simply be plain out of line, but because of the spanking Rowan gave me, it turns out to be excruciatingly painful.

Involuntarily, I let out a scream, arching my back to get him to release me, and when that doesn't work, grabbing his arm to twist away.

But he just holds me tighter, and the pain, the exquisite pain, buckles my knees. I drop to the floor, surprising both of us.

"What's this?"

I look up from the floor to see Hal, our burly doorman and all-around security guy, glaring at John Doe, who swallows hard while taking a step back.

Hal reaches for my arm and helps me to my feet, which, to be honest, doesn't feel much better. "Are you okay, Lu?" he asks.

I furiously smooth out my skirt, mortified by the whole thing. "Yes, yes, Hal. I'm fine. Everything's fine."

He glares at John Doe, then looks back at me. "Are you sure, Lu?"

Before I can answer, I hear the rustle of multiple layers of clothing. Without even looking, I know that Gwen has joined us.

Because, of course.

She clasps the member's arm, like he's her special date, and bats her eyelashes at him. "Everything good here?" she asks, like Hal and I are invisible.

John Doe takes a deep, indignant breath, ready to prey on her concern. "Well, Gwen. I'm not sure things are so good. I was just getting to know"—he points at me, like I'm a stain on the sidewalk—"this young lady here, but she was about as unfriendly as they come."

Hal and I look at each other with the understanding that we need to let Gwen take the lead on this. But I plan to let her know what really went down, first chance I get.

"I'll have a talk with Lu, don't worry," she says, glaring at me. "But for now, let's all get to where we need to be. Okay?" she asks cheerfully.

John Doe takes off down the hallway, and as soon as he's out of earshot, Gwen turns to Hal. "So. What did you see?"

He shakes his head. "I have to tell you, boss, it looked like the man was up to no good. Lu here was on the ground."

Gwen's eyebrows rise. "You were on the ground, Lu?"

I nod. "Yeah, you see, he grabbed me right where my last client spanked me. Hard."

Hal stifles a small grin and places a hand on each of our arms. "I'm getting back to work, ladies, since everything seems okay now."

"Thank you, Hal," I say.

Gwen places her hands on her hips and moves closer to me, so close I can see the flakes of mascara that have fallen off her lashes and onto her cheeks. "That member was upset," she spits at me.

I take a step back as if I can escape her vitriol. "He just… caught me so off guard. I'd just had a very intense session with Rowan, and this guy wanted me to turn around and head back to Room 21 with him. He said his name was John Doe, and he was just so gross—"

Gwen cuts me off, starting by pointing a finger right in my face. "I understand you need a break. But you must always, always make a member feel important. It doesn't matter whether you find him attractive or not. Not every member here looks like Max, Greyson, or Rowan. If someone wants your time, how he looks is not a factor in whether or not you accept. We can't do that to our clients. Do you understand?"

I nod. "Yes, I do, Gwen," I say quietly.

What's the point of arguing or even trying to discuss this with her? She's not going to listen.

"I'll smooth things over with him. You go get a shower and relax, okay?" she says.

Shower and relax. That's exactly what I needed to unpack the last couple hours of my life.

But about meeting with just any member of the club? Not sure about that.

Max, Greyson, and Rowan may have ruined me for anyone else.

---

I'M JUST OPENING my book to start studying, happy for something to take my mind off the day, when my cell rings. It's my friend from home, Melanie.

I flip my old phone open. Now that I have a little cash in the bank, I can get a fancy smartphone like everyone else. But I'm not going to. It's funny how when you want something, and then you can finally have it, you don't really want it anymore.

"Melanie!"

She's the one person from home I'm actually happy to hear from.

"Hey, girl. How's the big bad city?" she asks. I

can see her smiling, probably with a child on her hip.

She's the only person who didn't think I was crazy for going to Chicago to try my luck. And there's a good reason why.

Growing up, Mel wasn't quite the 'church girl' we were all brought up to be. Always a bit on the adventurous side, she was interested in boys from an early age. Unlike the rest of the girls in our parish, she didn't bother to hide her interest. A lot of disdain was flung her way, and she was called all the ugly names they call a girl. But I always stuck by her, even when my parents didn't want me to.

Guess that's why she sticks by me now.

But there's another reason, and I suspect it has to do with the fact that at the age of twenty-one, she already has three kids.

Yes. Three kids.

She got knocked up by local creep Jake Harlowe, in a situation where drugs and alcohol were involved, and which I've always suspected was not completely consensual. To make matters worse, in its infinite and 'compassionate' wisdom, the church pretty much made her marry him.

Pregnant with few or no job skills, what else could she do?

I was horrified, like I was witnessing the slow death of someone I loved.

Her mother practically dragged her down the aisle by the hair as she held her tears in, knowing that any life she'd hoped for was now out of her reach. Permanently.

I told her to run away, to do something, anything to avoid marrying him. But, for the first time in her life, she passively accepted everything happening around her, and went along with her parents' plans for her, which were really the church's plans.

Her fire died that day, and I think a little more dies with every day that passes. I hated how that happened to her, and now here she is, four years later with three babies, not to mention a gambler and philanderer of a husband.

The whole thing solidified my interest in getting out of our town, although I did so with more than a little guilt for leaving behind my friend.

"All is well here, Melanie, just about to dive into the books."

She sighs. And I feel like shit for her.

"I'll make it quick then, Luci. I'm organizing the youth dance at the church, and I would love if you came back for it. *Everyone* wants to see you."

Everyone? Who the heck is everyone?

"Oh, I don't know, Mel. I'm so busy with school and work."

The word *work* makes my heart speed up a bit. If she only knew.

Which she never will.

"Oh, Luci, c'mon. It will be so much fun. How can you not support the church that has done so much for you, and so much for me?"

*What?*

Please tell me she has not completely lost her mind or somehow come down with amnesia.

Does she not recall how she was essentially forced to marry someone she didn't like?

It's amazing how people can rewrite history. But maybe it's just as well. Blocks the most painful memories.

But I hadn't forgotten.

"I don't know, Mel. I... I support the church in other ways. I sent them money to help with the broken plumbing."

"Oh? You did? Gosh," she laughs weakly.

Ugh. Why did I just say that? I don't want more questions about my... life. Or finances, such as they are.

"Can I think about it? I just... well, you know

how important my bookkeeping certificate is to me, Mel. In fact, it's everything to me."

Surely, she can understand that.

And she does.

"Of course. I was just thinking it would be nice to see you," she says in a quiet voice. "Things here are… hard. Ya know?"

God help my dear friend. I know how things are for her. And my heart is breaking. Life has taken the wind out of her sails, and it isn't fair. It makes me so angry. And sad.

Which is why I won't let it happen to me.

———

# CHAPTER TEN

## MAX

CHRIST ALMIGHTY.

So that's what she looks like out of costume.

Lu joins the guys and me in the member lounge. We grab our usual corner seats, private enough for most kinds of conversations, but public enough to be seen. Which is important to us.

We know most everyone in the club. Some people we like and some we don't. We do business with a lot of the members, and from time-to-time issues crop up, like they do in any business dealing. Though it rarely happens, it's important for people to know not to fuck with us, because the way we resolve things is legendary. Sometimes we're nice, sometimes we're not. It comes with the territory.

I wave across the room at some of the guys from another syndicate, the Russian one that we're friendly with. They're decent men, and we've partnered on several… projects. I make a mental note to send them a bottle of scotch. See if they'll drink something other than vodka for a change.

Yeah, right.

And I turn my attention back to our lovely guest.

She's wearing a mid-thigh dress with a ruffled bottom swinging nicely around her long, toned legs as she crosses the room to us. Cute little platform shoes show off her red pedicure, and her luscious lips are coated in some glossy pink stuff, like icing on a cake.

One that I'd like to have a taste of. But there will be time for that, later.

Greyson, Rowan, and I want to have a little chat with her. Get to know her better. Find out what makes her tick, although we already know what makes her come, that's for damn sure. I have a feeling we have a new favorite girl, although the jury is still out. Rowan's the one holding us back. He's always the one holding us back.

The bottom line is that he's an asshole.

No one is ever good enough for him.

He's a successful, good-looking-enough guy, but hell if he doesn't have a major chip on his shoulder. Something to do with watching his dad get offed when he was a kid. He's told me the story a couple times over the years, but I have to say, it's so disturbing I do my best to forget it. Some shit I just don't need swirling around in my head. We all have our crosses to bear, but his is truly disturbing.

I will say, our business dealings have us doing some fucked up shit. We've had to off enemies on occasion over the years. But not in front of their goddamn kids. That's some seriously sick shit.

So while Rowan makes up his mind, I know what I want. I have for a long time.

I've resolved myself to a life spent with women whom I pay for companionship. Not that I don't have beautiful women interested in and sometimes throwing themselves at me. After all, I'm not a bad-looking guy, and I've got a fuck ton of money.

But the women I attract are not the ones I want to wake up next to on a long-term basis. Sure, they're beautiful and they fuck like champs, but I want a woman who's not looking for a walking wallet.

Unfortunately, women like that don't usually go for guys like me. Last woman I dated—I mean, really dated—hit the road when I told her what I did for a living. I wasn't going to fucking lie about it. Couldn't blame her, really. It's all good, though. When it comes down to it, I don't really give a fuck.

So, Greyson and I are still working on Rowan, who's basically being a prick by saying Lu was a goddamn virgin or something until he had his session with her the other day.

He's crazy. Gwen would never hire a virgin for the club. It's just not done. If Lu got some blood on him, it was probably her period, or he just fucked her too hard.

Something I would not put past him.

He needs to grow the hell up. And I say that with great affection. He's my best friend, after all. Our fathers were business partners a long, long time ago, and we basically grew up together.

Same with Greyson.

These guys are my brothers. We might all have different parents, but that doesn't matter. We laugh and fight like siblings. Always have, always will. We'd each take a bullet for the other. In fact, Greyson once did, ending up with a large indentation on his calf from where he was hit.

"Thank you for joining us, Lu," I say, taking the

chilled champagne from the silver bucket on our table and slowly filling a tall flute for her.

We guys don't drink that bubbly crap, preferring something harder. But women seem to like champagne, so it's a safe bet that Lu does too.

I hand her the flute and she brings it up to her mouth like she's smelling it at the same time. She takes a minuscule taste of it, then quickly licks her lips. It's almost as if…

No way.

But I have to ask. "Is this your first taste of champagne, Lu?" I ask.

She presses her lips together as a light blush washes over her face, and she sets the glass down. "N… no. I've had it plenty of times."

Holy shit. It *is* her first time.

I glance at the other guys and can tell they're thinking the same. We didn't get to where we are in the world by not being able to spot liars.

I don't like liars. But, if this is the worst thing Lu lies about, out of embarrassment or whatever, I can live with that.

We like that she's a little different from the other girls we meet. I mean, she comes off as sweet and naïve, which is surely all an act, but she does it so well, it has piqued our interest. Rowan's too. He's just being difficult.

"You've had it plenty of times?" he asks, not bothering to hide his skepticism.

I throw him a look, one he is perfectly familiar with. He better not scare her off with his intense craving for intimidation. I won't tolerate it.

But she just nods, clasping her hands over her crossed knee, swinging her top leg.

"Then you don't like it?" he asks.

She looks directly at him and while I could be wrong, I swear there's a flicker of annoyance in her eye, a subtle mood shift in someone who's not allowed to have mood shifts. She's working now, is on the clock so to speak, so is acting, playing a role not unlike what she does with us in Room 21.

Anyway, I like the little revelation. She knows she's being called out over something stupid.

No one can act one hundred percent of the time. We'll find out one way or another what makes her tick. Eventually. Today is just the start.

And yet, I do find it curious that someone her age, in her position, hasn't ever tasted champagne. There is more to this woman than meets the eye, and well, I always like a person who's misunderstood.

It's something I can relate to.

"Okay, fine," she blurts, "it's my first time."

"Nothing wrong with that," Greyson pipes up, always the peacemaker.

I nod. "That's right, Lu. But I do wonder how it is that a beautiful young woman like you has never been treated to bubbles?"

Most women who cross my path are champagne whores. When they see the guys and me, they buzz around like hungry little flies until we fill their greedy hands with the beverages of their choice.

I don't really mind. It's not like it strains my wallet or anything.

We're often surrounded by beautiful women, whether we pay them or not, like all good-looking guys with money probably are. We could seriously have IQs of ten and women would still flock to us. But that's about as far as it goes, at least for me.

After all, what father wants to see his daughter with a guy in the mob?

I sure as hell wouldn't.

Lu takes another sip of her champagne, this time slightly larger. The bubbles seem to surprise her, and she wipes a drop from her pretty bottom lip.

"Where I grew up, we didn't drink champagne. We didn't drink alcohol at all," she says matter-of-factly.

Okay. Now we're getting somewhere.

"What brings you to Chicago?" Greyson asks.

This seems to perk her up. Or at least give her some confidence. "I'm studying bookkeeping. I want to get my certificate," she says, pulling her shoulders back and raising her chin a little.

Okay, then. The girl's got some ambition. And pride. Nice.

"What do you think of Chicago so far? And what do you think about Club Sin?" Rowan asks with a faintly evil grin.

There he goes again, and I shoot him another look. So help me, if he fucks this up, I will kick his ass. He takes a dickish pride in putting people on the spot, but I need him to back off of Lu. I'm feeling protective of her, and won't hesitate to make that known, even with my old friend.

She tilts her head thoughtfully. "I like them both. Chicago is big and noisy. That takes some getting used to. And the club..."

Here's where she chooses her words carefully.

"The club is great. Although I did have a little run-in with a member the other day that wasn't too pleasant."

The moment she says that, she looks like she wishes she could retract her words. But I'm glad she told us. Because we don't tolerate that shit here.

I lean forward, elbows on knees, every inch of me tensing in a surprising visceral reaction. "What do you mean, Lu?" I ask, forcing my voice to remain merely curious rather than reactionary and rageful.

Any fucker who hurt her will pay. Big time.

She shifts in her seat in a way that would make me think she's just being a little shy if I didn't know better. But I can already tell she's about to talk about something that upset her.

And I don't like that.

After considering her words, she waves her hand around like *no big deal*. "Oh, he just wanted me to go with him when I… wasn't available."

A wave of anger runs down my spine. I don't like when I feel this way. Nothing good ever comes of it.

"Did he… touch you, Lu? Without your consent?" I ask.

She shrugs one shoulder. "Yeah. But security came. It all got straightened out."

Greyson presses his lips into a thin line, and I can see he feels as I do. A quick glance in Rowan's direction confirms the same. He might be difficult, but this is one area where there's no doubt about his priorities.

Damn right.

"What was the man's name, Lu?" I ask as nonchalantly as I can.

"Um, well, I'm not really sure. He told me his name was John Doe, but, you know, obviously it's not."

I look directly at her so she knows I'm not fucking around. "I want his name, Lu. I am serious." I try to keep the growl out of my voice. Not sure how successful I am.

She takes a deep breath, considering me, like she can't imagine anyone's actually taking up for her.

What is this girl's story? I've got to know. If I don't, I've no doubt it will haunt me to the end of my days.

"I… I told you. I don't know. You'll have to ask Gwen."

And there we have it. Fucking Gwen. Probably watched the whole goddamn thing and did nothing about it.

I have respect for the woman, or at least how she runs Club Sin, but she is pretty much motivated by the dollar and nothing else. She doesn't give a shit about anyone besides herself.

Which means that if someone hurts Lu, I can't count on Gwen to look out for her.

And that doesn't work for me.

I look at my watch. "Boys, it's time to get back to the office. But Lu, thank you for having a drink with us. It's a pleasure to get to know you better."

I'll find out more about what the hell happened between 'John Doe' and her later. I'll be letting him know, in no uncertain terms, that he needs to clean his act up. I know his type. He'll probably piss his pants when he realizes who he's up against. And after we let him know, he'll never harass a woman again.

Unless he's a complete idiot.

As she gets to her feet, I take her hand and gently kiss the back of it. I want to kiss so much more, but that time will come.

Fuck, what if she really had been a virgin? And that asshole Rowan was the one to pop her cherry?

Goddammit.

"Th... thank you. The champagne was very... nice. It's a good thing I live nearby and don't have to drive far, although I don't think I'll be doing much studying today," she says with a laugh that's about a hundred percent more confident than when our little meeting began.

Fuck if I don't want to take her with us. Protect

her from the bastard John Does out there and the greedy Gwens. Show her there are people who will look after her.

And feed her as much champagne as she would like.

# CHAPTER ELEVEN

## LUCI

I RE-TIE the sash on my new knock-off Diane von Furstenberg wrap dress, something I found on sale at Macy's, a store I've only ever been to one other time, when I first arrived in Chicago. It's so famous, and I'd heard so much about it, that it was one of the first things I wanted to see. I'd sneaked a peek at the Macy's Thanksgiving Day Parade a few times over the years, although my parents didn't approve, even if it was just a holiday parade. In fact, to this day I harbor a secret desire to visit New York. But I keep that to myself. It's bad enough I'm willing to give Chicago a try.

Today's job in Room 21 is acting out a bank

robbery. I'm kind of excited. No, scratch that. I'm really excited. I know I shouldn't be, and that my mother would say the stuff I've been doing at the club is condemning me to a life of fire and brimstone. But first, she'll never know, and second, I was well on my way toward believing all that talk about sinning and hell was questionable before I arrived in Chicago, anyway.

I mean, I've long wondered if some of my parents' Bible talk was over the top. Some of it just never made sense to me. I tried to understand it. I really did. I looked for all the signs that solidified the faith of everyone I knew. According to our church, these signs are all around us. Everywhere. But if that's the case, how come I never saw any of them? Was I not looking hard enough? Did God not want me to see them?

I'm just different. That's all I can chalk it up to, and now that I'm out of the small town I came from, I can see there are lots of people like me— people who want more of what the world has to offer.

To God's believers, those who are confident in their faith, more power to them. I'm honestly happy for them. But I just don't belong. I've suspected that for a long time, and now that I'm on a new path, I finally feel like I'm becoming whole.

That doesn't mean it's easy, though. Oh no.

Like what I do for the club. Some people might feel badly for me, submitting to men who want to use my body in ways only wicked, immoral women allow. They can feel that way all they want. But I know the money I make will help me stay on track with my life plans. And it goes without saying, I like the work. A lot.

It scares me to no end that I enjoy what I'm doing. It's exhilarating. I never know what to expect.

How my life has changed. And continues to.

Until recently, there was just one minimum-wage paycheck standing between my crappy little apartment and homelessness. Mine was a tenuous existence at best. In fact, it still is on some levels— it's just me and the dreams of a silly fool that keep me getting out of bed every day.

But I'll take tenuous any day, after what I came from.

After fixing my new dress, I give my thigh-high stockings—something else Gwen suggested I invest in—one more tug after I make sure no one's in the hall to see me adjusting myself, and round the corner to Room 21. Today's roleplay will be a fun one.

And as soon as I do, everything goes black.

I freeze in place, unsure what to do. Then, I try to scream, praying it's not the creep John Doe. But a hand clamps tightly over my mouth, preventing me from making a sound and even making it a little hard to breathe.

Oh god. Is this the end? Is this the punishment for my sinful ways?

It's funny, the minute things start going south, how we run back to God.

But this has nothing to do with God, I remind myself. And I'm the only one who can get myself out of this situation.

So I squirm and kick, and while I can't see a thing, I know there are at least four arms trying to control me. That doesn't bode well, being outnumbered, but at least a couple bodies increase my chances of hitting someone in my effort to try to free myself.

I scrunch my toes up in my high-heel shoes so they don't fall off, draw back, and kick one of my assailants as hard as I possibly can. I don't know where my blow lands, but I am suddenly restrained by two fewer arms, and the sound of someone moaning comes from the floor below me.

*Yes.*

"Cut it out, bitch," a voice growls in my ear. "You're only making it worse."

Worse? It can get worse?

He throws his arms around my upper body and lifts me from the floor, leaving my mouth uncovered.

I take advantage of this and scream. "Somebody help me!"

But no one does. No one. Which confuses me. The club is full of people, pretty much around the clock. Surely several people hear me. But no one comes to my aid, and in fact, I could swear I hear Gwen's laughter floating down the hall toward me.

"Gwen? Gwen, is that you?" I cry.

Why isn't she helping me? Why is nobody helping me?

Something doesn't add up. Where is Hal, the bouncer? He rushed to my aid the first time John Doe went after me.

I twist again, hoping to slip out of my assailant's hands, when I hear my dress rip.

Now, I'm getting angry. No one has the right to mess with me like this—

And then it dawns on me, at the same time the man dragging me down the hall speaks again. "Shut up, do you hear me? Shut up," he hisses in my ear.

I know this voice. And it's not creepy John Doe.

143

It might be Rowan. I'm not entirely sure. Maybe he'll speak again.

But why would Rowan try to abduct me?

I just had drinks with him and his friends.

While I'm trying to think through who's abducting me, why, and what I can possibly do about it, I'm half carried/half dragged like I weigh nothing I don't know how far, when a door swings open. I don't fall as much as I am *thrown* into a room, landing on my hands and knees. One of my shoes falls off and I feel for it, but of course I can't see anything and come up empty-handed.

"Stay where you are," someone growls as I try to get to my feet. "And keep the bag on."

I remain on my knees, assessing the thick, fluffy carpet beneath me as I grope for my missing shoe. I am clearly in one of the club's rooms. Which one, though, I have no idea.

"Is... is that you, Rowan? What's going on?" I ask quietly, hoping my tone will bring some calm to the situation.

I hear something rubbery crinkling and snapping from different ends of the room, and now it's clear there are more than just the two of us in here.

But how many?

"Can someone please tell me what's going on?" I plead with a lame laugh, trying to keep things light. As if I'm not bothered by being abducted at my place of work on the way to Room 21 by someone or *someones* who put a black bag over my head? Like I'm cool with it all. Really. No big deal. Happens to me every day.

*Not.* Last I checked, this is not part of the deal.

Or is it?

"Gentlemen, I think we've stumbled onto something far more valuable than anything we expected," another voice says.

Wait. Is that Max?

For heaven's sake.

"I think you're right. Look at her. She's quite lovely."

Okay. That's Greyson.

Right?

"Hey, why aren't her hands zip tied? Can someone take care of that?"

I don't think so.

Shoes brush over the soft carpet, heading in my direction. I cross my arms tightly so no one can force me to do anything I don't want, but in one swift move, someone has my arms behind my back, strapping my wrists together, cutting into my skin with unforgiving plastic ties. When he's done and begins to move away, and I hear him in front of me, I kick one foot out with all the force I can. I'm not sure I'll hit anything, but I sure hope I do.

And I do.

"Ow, shit," he howls. "Goddammit, she got me again."

Laughter fills the room and I smile underneath my hood, glad for a moment that they can't see my face. "Man, you're gonna be covered with bruises when all is said and done."

"Yeah, real fucking funny, asshole."

I'm sure—well, pretty sure—I'm in a room with Max, Greyson, and Rowan. Which is fine. Completely fine, although I don't know why they had to go through the drama of abducting me in the hallway.

And while it sounds like them, it also doesn't. Their voices are muffled, somehow.

"Wh… who are you? All of you?" I ask, wondering to what extent I'm supposed to play along.

My question is ignored as footsteps brush over the plush carpet again toward where I'm sitting. A large hand wraps around my upper arm to the point of pain, and I am yanked to my feet. Since I am still wearing only one shoe, I'm completely off balance.

And probably look ridiculous.

"You want this hood taken off, pretty girl?" a voice asks right in my ear.

That would be nice.

But I decide not to be a smart aleck. "Yes. I do. Please."

The fabric that's been around my head since I was grabbed in the hallway starts to shift around.

Thank goodness.

"Close your eyes," he says.

And the hood is lifted.

# CHAPTER TWELVE

## LUCI

EVEN THOUGH MY hood is removed, I still don't get to see anything. Of course not. I'm silly to hope otherwise.

My abductors are too smart for anything like that. The second I try to look around the room, my eyes adjusting to the light after being immersed in darkness for so many minutes, a blindfold replaces it, is tied behind my head, and then is adjusted over my eyes—for comfort? For security? I can only guess.

So much for seeing anything. But it is better than the hood, by a lot. The hood was just creepy. Hot. Smelly. Stifling. It left me panicky and fearful.

The blindfold is... sexy, I think is the word to describe it. I mean, I'm still not in control of... anything, really, but it's somehow not as aggressive, and is certainly more comfortable. I can breathe easier.

I kick off my one high-heeled shoe so I am on two feet again, and the balance gives me courage. While my hands are tied behind my back, and I can't see anything, I can hold my head up and pull my shoulders back.

"Are you going to tell me who you are?" I ask again.

Something rubbery touches my cheek, and I jerk my head away. What is that?

"You don't need to know, little girl," a man whispers in my ear, so close I can feel his warm breath.

And then I feel it again. The rubber. And I can smell it too. It's chemical-y, like a Halloween mask.

Wait? Are these people wearing Halloween masks? What for? I'm blindfolded.

"Is... is that a mask on your face?" I ask, not expecting an answer.

A finger runs down my cheek, and I realize that, too, feels like rubber.

"Of course, we have masks on. Gloves too. We

don't want evidence, do we, young lady?" he croons.

I don't speak until the finger stroking me becomes a hand around my neck. The man yanks, tilting my chin up so my head falls back. He tightens his fingers. Fortunately, in spite of the pressure, I can still breathe—so nice of him—but I wheeze because he still manages to restrict my air flow.

"Wh... what are you doing?" I rasp.

I can knee him in the crotch. But why? What good will that do? I'm blindfolded and my hands are tied. I might be able to run, but where?

He scoffs and releases my neck, running his hand down my chest to grab one of my breasts. At first, he strokes me with his open palm, and though I shouldn't enjoy it, it feels nice, even through the fabric of my dress. I drop my chin back to a comfortable position and take a big inhale.

"Yeah, there you go, little girl, much better, huh?"

I nod in spite of myself. I mean, I still don't quite know what's going on. Is this the scene I am supposed to play? The one Gwen set up for me? If so, why was I left in the dark about the details?

But I guess that's the point.

And what the hell am I doing, anyway? I came to Chicago to take courses, not hang out with perverts and sinners. What kind of girl am I if not a horrible hypocrite?

Something I've been asking myself for as long as I can remember.

I stiffen under the man's touch, his palm now off my breast, his fingers having reached inside my dress to rest around a nipple. The plastic gloves are strange on my skin but also exciting. They're smooth and cool. They kind of tickle.

Wait. This is not arousing. Or rather, it's not supposed to be.

If anything I learned growing up is true, this is supposed to feel dirty, a man touching me who I don't know, don't have a relationship with, don't love, and am not married to. What I am doing is wrong on every single level except one.

The one where I like it.

It might be dirty. Humiliating. Sinful. Downright wrong.

But I like the fear. The humiliation. The shame. The sin.

I want this, even though I don't know what kind of woman it makes me.

"The bed."

I turn toward a different voice, familiar but

muffled. I must be with the three guys. Who else could it be?

"What? Excuse me?" I ask.

While the man with his hand on my breast stands on one side of me, someone else approaches me on my other. Both my arms now have strong hands holding them.

I'm not going anywhere. Well, anywhere these men don't want me to.

"I said, get over to the bed."

"How can I move over to the bed? I can't see anything."

"And that's why we're helping you, little girl," the new guy says.

I take just a few steps forward until my knees bump a soft mattress. The guys turn me around and with a small push, I am sitting.

The one who was playing with my nipple pulls open the top of my wrap dress and pushes down the lace cups of my bra. Cool air flows over my bare breasts, and my nipple hardens as a result. I want to shrink back, unaccustomed as I am to being bare chested in front of anyone, much less strange men, but I fight the urge.

"Look at those pretty little tits," someone says from across the room.

My thoughts are whipping around between

guilt and pleasure, and I am dizzy because of it. I also like that they are admiring my breasts. I want them to like them. I want them to like all of me.

That will give me power.

Hands reach under my thighs where I am sitting and yank me to the very edge of the bed, almost to the point where I am barely still sitting on it and think I'm about to fall off. Then, someone reaches under my wrap dress, ripping my panties off so fast I barely know what's happening.

I hear a zipper open, and I flip-flop between being petrified and thrilled.

I am such a bad girl.

"Open them," someone growls.

I move my head toward the sound, as if I might see the person making the request. But of course, I can't.

"Open them?" I repeat in a weak voice.

Like, open my thighs? So they can see my... everything?

I can't do that. I can't let these men drool over my most private parts. And now that they're shaved, there is no hiding. Anything. They may have already seen me, but that doesn't mean I am comfortable with it.

Regardless, I spread my knees apart. Just a

little. Because the drop of moisture running out of me is proof that I like this.

"More."

I acquiesce another inch or two until one of the guys plants his hands on my knees and shoves them open, as far as they go, until it actually hurts, pushing up against the limits of my flexibility. The movement throws me onto my back, on top of my restrained hands, which is awfully uncomfortable. No one seems to care.

I'm lying back with my behind basically hanging off the edge of a bed, with the hands of two men holding me so far open that everything between my legs, including what is dripping out of me and running toward the crack of my butt, is on view.

Again, fear, humiliation, and exhilaration run through me so fast it hurts my head. I want to scream *help*. But exactly what kind of help I need, I'm not exactly sure.

Do I want rescuing?

Or do I want relief!

Could they be the same thing?

"Look at that pretty cunt, boys, right there before us."

Oh my god.

A finger drags up my slit, and I shiver.

"Are you a whore, little girl?" someone asks, his hand pressing on my forehead, pushing me back into the bed.

I squirm, trying to get comfortable lying on my tied hands.

"I… I don't… know," I stumble.

Was I? Was I a whore?

"You wanna be a whore, baby?" he asks.

Oh god. That's the question. I mean, that about sums it up.

Do I want to be a whore?

"I… do you want me to be?" I ask, unsure of the right answer.

The man holding my head down gets close to my ear. "Yeah. And I think you want to be, too."

I hear trousers unzip right next to my head, and a velvety penis runs over my face. It slaps against my lips until I turn my head and take part of it into my mouth.

I've never sucked a penis. But I part my lips and taste it, wet and salty on the tip, and then I open wide.

"Mmmm, little girl. She likes it. She likes sucking my cock," the man murmurs, pushing deeper inside my mouth, but just a little.

"Hold them for me," the guy between my legs says. The hands holding me open shift.

I feel someone's breath on my privates, and I wonder if he's going to lick me down there. Can he do it while still wearing his mask?

I take another inch of the penis in my mouth, and find I am enjoying the hardness of it, the overall rigidity, but also the warm smoothness of the skin.

"Ouch!" I scream, spitting the penis out when one of the men, I assume the one *not* holding my knees, takes an open palm and slaps me between my legs right on my privates. The pain isn't excruciating, but it's such an unexpected surprise that my entire body convulses in response.

What the hell is that all about?

The hand instantly returns, smoothing my flesh and everything in between the lobes that protect my insides.

"Such fat pussy lips," he murmurs, stroking them.

Then, he takes his fingers and opens me like pages in a book, and that time, that one time, I want to crawl away and die in shame. But of course, I can't. All I can do is lie there, trapped, betraying myself as more fluid leaks from my opening.

"She loves it," he says, running a finger from my behind to my opening. Sucking sounds follow.

Did he just taste me off his fingers?

Oh my god.

Such a filthy man.

And he's just getting warmed up. "Do you want to be fucked, little girl? Do you want my cock in your tight little pussy?"

How do I answer that?

"I… I… um, I don't know."

I want it but I don't want it. It makes no sense.

"Can you say it? Repeat after me?"

I take a deep breath. "I… I guess so."

"Say it, sweetness. Say you want me to fuck your pussy."

Oh. No. I don't say words like that. Or at least, I never have.

"I… can't," I say, my breath quickening as one and then two fingers slide inside of me, making a crazy motion that makes me feel like I need to pee.

Is this what people do? Is this what I've been warned about all my life? Because it makes no sense to deny it. Why stay away from something that feels so good, I ask myself for the umpteenth time.

Doesn't sound very godly to me.

A hand presses on my forehead again. It's not uncomfortable, but it is unmistakably dominant and meant to show me who's in charge, and that it isn't me.

"Say it," he growls.

"I... I want you to fuck"—I was saying it, those horrible words, the words of sinners—"fuck my... pussy."

Oh god. I said it. I said the words of sinners, asking for what sinners want.

Because I am a sinner myself.

I squeeze my eyes shut behind the blindfold, as if that will bleed off some of my disgrace.

Fuck.

Pussy.

I've never uttered those words before.

But I like them. I want to say them again. So I do.

"Yes, please, fuck my pussy," I say through heavy, immoral breaths.

Everything about me is sinful. Just how I've always known.

I hear the nightstand drawer open and close and then a condom wrapper tears open. Then, someone is poised at my entrance—the entrance to my *pussy*. And while I'm not sure who it is, he's about to *fuck* me.

It's wrong, it's wrong, it's wrong. And I want it so badly I know I'll die if I don't get it.

He plunges inside me in one swift movement, and I scream from the stretch, the stretch of my *pussy*.

I like that word. I like having a word for my sinful place, which is also my holy place.

All men want it, right? That's what I've always been taught. And if they want it so badly, how can it be sinful?

If you ask me, that's holy.

And this man, his hardness strokes my insides, and as someone holds my legs open and another holds my head down, I can only move my arms, so I grab handfuls of the bed linens beneath me for purchase. The man glides in and out like we were made for each other, aided by the slickness gathered between my legs.

And then the tickle starts. That's all I can think to call it. Beginning in my core, it flickers at first, like a campfire struggling to ignite, the flames licking around, deciding whether they want to become something bigger.

And then they grow, like the pressure inside me, and something pulses in a steady rhythm, weak at first but quickly becoming strong, until my body is wracked with spasms. My head breaks free of the hand on it, and I lift and slam it back down on the bed over and over, grateful something soft is under me because I know I can't stop.

My pussy contracts like it has a mind of its own, taking me on a ride that leaves me thrashing and screaming. Over the noise in my ears and in my mind, I hear the men making approving noises, enjoying the fuck just as much as I do.

And then the man slams into me one more time, so hard he drives me back on the bed, and I shriek from the force and the combination of pain and pleasure, and he growls and then yells, so loudly I am sure they hear us outside our room.

And I don't care. I just want it again.

# BOOK II

# CHAPTER THIRTEEN

## LUCI

IT'S NOT easy walking down a dark street in a long dress and high heels, shoulders and back bared to a chilly breeze, one that normally calls for a coat or wrap or something else that's warm.

But I don't want to put my ratty jeans jacket over the long, silk halter dress the guys got me. And I also don't want to park close enough to their house that anyone might see me exiting my junky car.

So, I drive past Greyson's house two times until I'm certain which home in this tony neighborhood is his, and then up a hill and around a corner with the brilliant plan of walking back to the party he invited me to.

A party that, in truth, I am not actually allowed to attend.

Since I started working at Club Sin, from the time I was the cleaning person to now, working exclusively in Room 21, it has been drilled into my head that seeing clients outside the club is strictly forbidden.

But, having guessed my size perfectly, Greyson bought me this amazing teal-blue dress, he says because it matches my eyes. So, I figure I can risk my cushy setup to wear it once. Just once, to see where he lives, and to spend time with the guys outside Club Sin. I'm breaking rules, something I've been doing so much lately I'm not even sure anymore where the rules start and stop, because I'm just plowing ahead trying to figure things out on my own. Rules haven't served me well to this point. Maybe they never will.

Greyson also asked me to help him host his party. Which I thought was strange but sweet.

*Me*, host a party? He has no idea about the kinds of parties I'm used to—the ones with cake and punch, and shy conversation between boys and girls, all zealously overseen by hawkeyed parents.

He has assured me that all I have to do, basically, is be his date. Hang out with him, chat with his guests, and help make sure everyone has a drink.

He says it will be just a few close friends, including Max and Rowan, and that I'll be perfectly comfortable. I wonder for a moment if this is another role play no one's telling me about beforehand. And if it is, that's fine. I'm ready this time.

I'm ready for anything, actually.

The guys have taken to fucking me—I'm using that word fairly freely now—individually and sometimes all together. They tell Gwen they like me, which she happily reports back, taking credit as if she was the one dressing up and having sex with them.

I don't place a lot of credence in the information she shares. The three men are handsome and rich and can have any woman or women they want. I am under no illusion I am anything to them but a toy, a fun distraction to pass the time until they tire of me and move on to someone else. I haven't been around the club all that long, and there are a lot of things I don't know about life. But I am not stupid.

And it's fine. Really. I enjoy the attention, the

sex, and the money. Through it all, I cling to my thrifty lifestyle, my plan, and save the bulk of my earnings. I consider myself lucky to have gotten this break.

That is, when I'm not thinking about the sinfulness of it. Which is less and less as time passes.

Walking up the pathway to Greyson's front door, shivering, I'm careful not to break my neck on the brick pavers, barely lit up in the night time darkness. That's all I need, for my heels—another gift from Greyson—to catch between them and catapult me and my perfect dress head first onto his manicured front lawn.

I pause before pressing his doorbell, trying not to mentally assess all the things I am doing wrong at that moment, and hoping against hope to hide my shivering until I warm up and am comfortable again. Maybe I'll even have a glass of champagne—or two. When I tried it before, it sent a wave of heat through me that left a light sweat on my forehead. I'd welcome that warmth right now.

Greyson's door flies open, and I gasp, with any luck not too loudly. He's just *that* perfect in his black bowtie. "Here she is," he proclaims, making me feel like a million dollars, taking my hand and ushering me in the door. "Where's your coat, darling?" he asks, rubbing his hands over my shoulders to warm me.

I wave off his question, something I'm learning to do quite skillfully. Someone asks a question you don't want to answer?

Smile, laugh, and just don't respond.

"Oh, I left it in the car. Didn't want to forget it, you know?" I say breezily, gobbling up his touch and wishing he could rub more than just my shoulders.

*Down girl.*

He throws a casual arm around my shoulder, and for a moment, I feel like *his girl.* I am important to him. He likes me and even loves me at least a little. He looks good and I look good and everything in the world is perfect. Forever.

"Where is everybody?" I ask, looking around his cavernous entryway and the winding staircase beyond.

I've never been in a house like this before. No big surprise there. The walls are covered in beautiful, polished wood, hung with huge paintings, mostly what I guess would be called 'modern' art. I'm not really sure. In the middle of the tiled black and white floor, which kind of reminds me of a checkerboard, there is a large round table with an enormous arrangement of flowers.

I didn't think guys had flowers in their houses.

Maybe it's a rich-person sort of thing?

So, this is how these guys live. The members of Club Sin. I tried to imagine what their homes would be like. But in all my imagination, I never pictured anything quite like this. It reminds me of a magazine I used to see at the public library for architects or some such.

"The guys are in the library, this way," he says, gently directing me toward two large, closed doors.

He has a *library*? In his *house*?

"Great," I say, fake-cheerfully.

"The other folks will arrive in a bit. We'd like to talk to you first."

His words hit my stomach like a sledgehammer, and my first physical reaction is to either vomit, run back out the door and leave, or both.

Both would be better, even though I'm finally starting to warm up.

But we pass through the heavy wooden library doors, and he pushes them closed behind us with a soft *click*.

I find Max and Rowan, dressed equally formally and looking equally handsome, standing by the fireplace, holding rocks glasses containing some sort of amber liquor.

Scotch, I think it is. I think that's what they drink.

"Here she is," Max says graciously, kissing the back of my hand and then the side of my neck.

Rowan, true to form, just raises his glass to me in greeting. "Heya," he mumbles.

Probably the least friendly person I've come across in my life. But the twinkle in his eye gets me every time. And then there's the way he is when we have our clothes off, doing… adult things. The things I love doing.

Every time I look at him, I blush.

Actually, anytime I look at any of the guys I blush, an unforgiving heat washing over me, giving away all my dirty, filthy thoughts.

Greyson takes my hand and leads me to a cushy velvet sofa, which I sink into so deeply I'm not sure how I'll get back up.

I'm sitting slightly sideways to minimize wrinkles to my dress. Greyson turns so his knee's touching mine, and he looks directly at me.

God, he's amazing. All the guys are, actually. Even Rowan. Now that I've been around him several times, I think of him as a pineapple— prickly on the outside but sweet and juicy inside. He's got a chip on his shoulder but seems like a good guy underneath it all.

Max, so cute with his mass of curls, confided in me in a moment of uncharacteristic vulnerability that he thought he'd die alone. When I probed, he was vague, but I was pretty sure he meant in terms of a romantic partner.

Does he really think no one could fall in love with him? Crazy.

Not that I would. No, not at all.

And then there's Greyson, the quietest. Even though he's younger than the other two, he's got the start of some distinguished crow's feet in the outer corners of his eyes and a bit of gray peeking through the dark hair on his temples.

Someday I'm certain he'll be one of those head-turning 'older gentlemen' that the ladies drool over.

"We have something to discuss with you, Lu," he says, snapping me out of my reverie, his hot, hungry gaze drifting over me as he speaks.

Ugh. I don't stand a chance against him. Any of them.

"What's up? What did you want to talk about?" I ask, uneasily eyeing each guy, my hands folded in my lap to hide my nerves.

But they just smile back at me, relaxed in their big, comfy chairs that probably each cost more than all the furniture in my parents' house together.

Rowan takes a sip of his drink. "We've had a talk with Gwen," he starts.

Gwen? Oh, this can't be good.

Nothing good ever comes of a conversation when Gwen's name is mentioned, at least not in my experience.

He continues. "We've discussed having you exclusively. As in, only the three of us can see you at the club."

Oh. That's... interesting.

Actually, it's more than interesting. I like the idea. At least I think I do.

"What... what did Gwen say?" I ask.

Max leans forward in his chair, elbows on knees. "She supports it, fortunately. Although, it's not like she has much choice." He laughs and sits back, pleased with himself.

In fact, Rowan and Greyson also wear the smiles of men used to getting their ways. None of them are surprised in the least that Gwen bowed to their wishes. They knew all along she'd say yes.

Even if she didn't want to.

But who am I to complain? I get to hang out with these guys a bit longer, and it sure beats cleaning cum.

"Sounds like a win-win situation," I say, like it's a business transaction.

Which, for them, I suppose it is.

For me, I'm not so sure.

The guys look at each other. "Well, I guess we weren't expecting such a lackluster response. But we'll take it," Greyson says with a laugh, giving me a peck on the cheek. "Now that we've gotten that out of the way, shall we join the party?"

The party. I nearly forgot.

We rise, and Greyson pulls open the library double doors to reveal a party in full swing. Where did all these people come from?

I inch up to him. "I thought you said there would be only a few people," I say quietly.

My mouth is getting drier by the second, and my stomach flutters so wildly I have to place my hand on my abdomen. Will I have to talk to these people? What will I say? That I am taking a book-keeping course?

What could be more boring?

I glance toward the front door, where guests keep pouring in. Maybe when none of the guys is looking, I can sneak away later... claiming I had a headache or something.

But Greyson links his fingers through mine, securing my fate, and even though I now know

I can't escape, which alarms me, his warm hand feels good in mine, like some sort of security blanket. My thoughts of escape slowly slip away.

I hope he doesn't plan on letting me go.

"Oh, these are friends and associates of ours. Just a little gathering," he says, explaining what I consider to be hordes of people. He waves across the room at someone.

"Your associates?" I ask, remembering Gwen's vague explanation of what they do for a living.

He turns and his gaze locks on mine. "We are one of the local syndicates. In the old days, people called us the *mob*," he says with a dismissive laugh. "But that term is quaint nowadays. We're the strongest in the region. The others pretty much defer to us. Most of the time, anyway," he says, grimacing as some new men pass through the front door.

"Um, syndicate? Mob? What exactly does that mean?"

I think it means crime. But I want to be sure.

Am I in a houseful of criminals? My evening just went from unfamiliar and intimidating to downright terrifying.

He furrows his brow like he's puzzled. "You don't know?"

I shake my head slowly. "Is it like in the movies?"

He smiles. "Nah, that's all Hollywood bullshit. Organized crime is nothing like that in real life. It's much more nefarious and deadly. Now, shall we mingle?"

# CHAPTER FOURTEEN

## GREYSON

THOSE MEN HAD BETTER NOT COME near Lu.

I am a patient man. Much more so than my business partners, Max and Rowan. I'm the calm, collected part of the team, and they are goddamn lucky to have me. If not for my ability to finesse some of the situations we've been in, they'd both be dead men.

And normally, when I see our sometime business partners Vadik, Kir, and Niko Alekseev from the Russian syndicate, I'm pleased. They're good guys and Max, Rowan, and I have partnered with them many times over the years. We call them the 'Bratva Brothers,' not that they'll ever know that.

It's just the inside name the guys and I use for them.

When they arrive at my party and Kir's gaze wanders toward me, he nods in greeting from across the room. But it takes less than a second for him to notice Lu. And he doesn't look away from her.

I get it. She's beautiful in a simple, girl-next-door sort of way, and I don't say that meaning to patronize or condescend. In my day to day, and really, any guys working in syndicates, we don't meet women like Lu. They just don't cross our paths. We get a different type of woman—someone who's more worldly and street smart. Beautiful in a different sort of way.

If there is anything I like in life, it's a little variety. And Lu offers that in spades. But it's not only her appearance that's different.

It's her innocence. Sure, she tries to act like she's been around the block, lying about silly things like having tried champagne. And who the hell knows why she arrived at my house on a cold evening with no coat. But it's clear as day to the guys and me that she's just now coming into her own. Club Sin has been the perfect place for her to explore that, and we are the perfect members to guide her through her transformation. I don't know where she started—she's private about that shit—but I will know at some point.

Because I want to know everything about her. Even the stuff she's ashamed of. I want to teach her she has nothing, and I mean fucking *nothing*, to ever be ashamed of. That's how perfect she is.

Of course, she doesn't know we see that in her. It's pretty clear she thinks she's pulling one over on us—not in a bad way, she's just trying to save her pride. Which is exactly why we don't call her out on it.

At least, we haven't yet.

Hell yes, we all want to learn more about this woman. Curiosity is driving us crazy. Keeping us up at night.

On one hand, she's so damn sensual and responsive. But on the other, she doesn't drink or swear. At least she didn't until we guys fed her champagne and taught her to say *fuck* and *pussy* to give her a little taste of how bad girls live.

But we know not to ruin a good thing. She's... *unspoiled*, and we have no interest in tarnishing that. Why would we? It's one of the things we like best about her.

And fucking her is pure heaven. There is just something about her flawless skin, and the way she squirms when I'm stroking in and out of her pussy

—well, I've had to jerk myself every night before I go to sleep, so much so that my pump hand is starting to get sore.

We've not known her long, of course, but she is just so... precious that I am barely able to tolerate anyone else—with the exception of Max and Rowan—looking at her with more than just a passing glance.

So, it figures that Kir, having noticed Lu, makes a beeline across the party toward us, his gaze locked on her the entire time, his brothers just behind, nodding and shaking hands with acquaintances. Lu's been holding my hand in a death grip, clearly feeling out of her element. But I want her to know she belongs anywhere we guys say she does. So, to make her more comfortable, and to send the message to Kir that, as much as I like the guy, he'd better not come *too* close, I sling an arm around her waist and pull her tight to me.

She glances up at me, a look of surprise crossing her face quickly followed by one of gratitude. She blinks her speckled eyes, which reflect the killer blue dress I got her, and smiles, her pink lips stretching into a small but lovely curve.

If there weren't a hundred guests in my home at that moment, I'd bend her right over the table in my center hall, lift up her long dress, and slide my…

"Greyson. Good to see you," Kir says, shaking my hand and trying, but failing, not to stare at Lu.

I slap Kir on the back with my free hand, wishing on some sort of uncivilized level I could smack him harder and pull some alpha male bullshit that would make me feel better for a split second. "Glad you could make it. It's always great to see the Alekseev brothers."

"And it's always great to be in this incredible house, Grey," Vadik says, shaking my hand after Niko.

There's no doubt they've all noticed Lu at this point, but Vadik and Niko are more discreet in their admiration than their brother Kir. "Who's your lovely friend?" he croons, taking her hand and lifting it to his lips.

My arm involuntarily tightens around Lu's waist, a movement not lost on her. She politely but firmly draws her hand back, resting it over mine, and lifts her chin.

God bless her.

"I'm Lucinda," she says in a firm, confident voice.

*Lucinda?*

Well, shit.

"Lucinda," Kir says like he's running his tongue up her body. "Beautiful name. For a beautiful lady."

"Thank you."

"And what is it you do, my dear?" he asks.

Okay. Fine. He's digging. Trying to find out what kind of girl she is and whether she's available.

"I'm a student," she says proudly.

That's my girl.

Kir bows his head to her. "Beautiful *and* smart."

It's not lost on Lu that Kir and his two brothers are good looking guys. Tall, buff as hell, and covered in tattoos...

*Fuck me.* Am I jealous?

What a little bitch I am.

A moment later, before I can reconcile this strange feeling and relax my clenched jaw, a hand lands on my shoulder, startling me. "Well, if it isn't the Alekseev brothers," Rowan booms, extending his hand to each.

Did he notice what I did and swing by to protect his claim?

Christ, what animals we men are.

Regardless, I grab the opportunity to escape. Of course, with Lu.

Fuck, I don't like being jealous. It's a sign of weakness, and I am not a weak man.

But I can't help it. I'm okay with Max and Rowan wanting her, coveting her, even owning her. But not any other man or men. No, that I can't abide.

"Who are they?" Lu asks when we'd stepped to the side of the room with a fresh champagne for her and a bourbon for me.

I study her face for a moment, starting where her blonde hair is pulled tightly back from her face, down her smooth forehead to her arched brows, past those damn glittering eyes, to her perfectly straight nose and then to her pink lips, delightfully plump and symmetrical. Almost too perfect, really.

And her tits in that silk halter dress I got her, my god. The teardrop shape of them is perfectly visible, thanks to my selection, and her nipples have been hard and poking through the thin fabric since she arrived at my door.

Coatless. Does she not have a goddamn coat?

I know what I'll be purchasing next time I shop for her. I've got to teach her to ask for what she needs.

When I get it together and stop staring at her, I consider her question.

*Who were those men?*

Simple question. Complicated answer.

But I don't see myself lying. She deserves better.

"They're from the Russian syndicate."

Her brows rise. "Is that like the syndicate you work for?"

I think for a moment. How to explain who I am to a woman like Lu escapes me.

I will just have to hope she understands.

"Yes. Absolutely. They have businesses they run, mostly owned by Russians, just like we have businesses that we... inherited from our families. We do a lot of... things, Lu. Things some people might not approve of."

I am suddenly strangely self-conscious. I don't want her to think poorly of me. I respect her so much, and I want the same from her.

She looks over my shoulder at the milling guests, all decked out in their finest, smiling and glad-handing, seeing and being seen. "What about them?" she asks, gesturing with her chin.

I nod slowly. "Nearly all business associates. In one way or another."

Her hand shakes, almost imperceptibly. I only notice because the champagne in her glass moves in tiny waves. "So, everyone here is in... organized crime? Or something like that?"

Okay. She gets it.

I look out over the crowd of people, most of whom Max, Rowan, and I have known for years. Community leaders, elected officials, mom-and-pop business owners, high-rollers. We know them all.

"For the most part, Lu, yes," I say matter-of-factly.

"Are they... dangerous? Are we in danger?" she asks with wide eyes.

Fuck if I'd let anything happen to her. If she doesn't know that yet, she soon will.

"There are times, Lu, when things get dangerous. Now is not one of them. Everyone is getting along fine, business is perking along. But keep in mind that, no matter what happens, I will never, ever let anything happen to you. Nor will Max or Rowan."

I run a finger down her temple, then caress her cheek with my palm. With a finger under her chin, I lift her face to mine. "You are special to me, Lu. Very special. Same with the other guys." I bend to kiss her and after a moment of hesitation, she melts into me, her hand wandering up to my chest while I pull her to me, my hand on the small of her back. When I stop, she sighs.

We've been interrupted.

"Hey, you bastard."

We whip around to see Rowan grinning, ear to ear.

"Hi," Lu says.

Rowan takes her hand and starts to lead her away. "You know I love you, Grey, but you can't bogart our girl all night. I've got to have a couple spins on the dance floor with her before it's too late."

She laughs and hands me her champagne, leaving me standing there, looking after her, like a goddamn teenage boy at his first dance.

# CHAPTER FIFTEEN

## LUCI

I'M LYING if I don't admit the whole evening at Greyson's is one big rush of emotion, from being nervous, to flattered that the guys want me all to themselves, to finding out I'm surrounded by likely criminals, to spending a night of delicious, sinful passion with Max, Rowan, and Greyson.

It's scary, confusing, and exhilarating. I don't understand how or why I feel this way.

I also feel like a sinner... and an angel at the same time. When I'm with these guys, I'm smart, beautiful, seductive, desirable. And I do terrible, dirty things.

So much so that these handsome, rich men want me all to themselves.

Although there's the small detail of what they do for a living. I'm not sure yet how to reconcile that. Maybe I never will.

When I wake up the next morning in Greyson's house, the guys are gone. I would have loved to laze around in bed for half the day, like some sort of lady of leisure, but today's my day off from Club Sin, and I have to get in as much study time as possible. Plus, I'm meeting Charleigh later at our favorite coffee shop.

So, on the drive home, in the crappy little car I parked a couple blocks from Greyson's, I replay the evening like a movie reel on loop, pausing at certain highlights.

After meeting the guys who Greyson refers to as the Bratva Brothers, Rowan sweeps me away for a dance, followed by Max. The guys don't let me spend a moment alone the whole evening, and while some of the women there look me up and down with disdain—I guess I'm just not as glamorous as they are—I've never felt so special. My cheeks ache from smiling. The arms around my waist, the hands that grip mine, the fingers that brush the thin silk covering my behind, and the lips that touch my cheek are casual and yet intentional, off-hand but deliberate, like we've known each other forever. And yet each touch is achingly unique, confusingly new.

They cast some sort of spell over me. Just like my mother said the sinners would, if I were not careful.

Guess she was right.

And I couldn't be more excited about it. A whole new world has opened up for me and I plan to gobble up every last morsel of affection these guys have to offer, for as long as it lasts.

Because it won't last. I'm certain of it.

After the last guest leaves, Greyson crooks his finger in my direction. I kick off my high heels and follow him, with Max and Rowan just behind. I don't know what they have in store for me, but my senses are buzzing in preparation for the surprises they always deliver.

In spite of all I've done with the guys, I am struck with shyness on entering Greyson's bedroom. There is something so intimate about being in an actual home, specifically someone's bedroom, as opposed to the Club, which I hadn't realized has an air of the impersonal about it. In the club, I was to remain *somewhat* detached from the guys. Seeing them in their element provides an entirely new perspective.

It's a bit like meeting them all over again. I am grateful for the opportunity to see them this way, and I want to show it.

So, I untie my dress from behind my neck, open the side zipper, and let the beautiful silk slither to the floor, where it pools around my bare feet. All I am left wearing is a skimpy G-string with barely enough fabric to cover my sex, the skinny straps reaching around my hips where they intersect with another that runs down my crack.

I kick the dress aside and slowly turn. First, to let the guys have a complete view of how I am offering myself to them, and second, to look at each as they circle me like a den of ravenous lions. I am in the middle, the spoke to their wheel, the center of their attention, the temptress of all their weaknesses.

It's powerful, so powerful to be looked at like I am, with those hungry eyes. I am their lamb, voluntarily giving myself up to slaughter. I want them to devour me, leaving nothing about me unchanged.

I drop to my knees and beckon Greyson the way he just beckoned me up the stairs. He slowly approaches, and when he is right in front of me, he places his hands on my head. I grab for his belt buckle and fly and through his shirt tails pull out the cock I am getting to know so well but which I've never had in my mouth.

I might not be all that experienced, but that doesn't mean I'm not learning how things work and what men like.

By the time I wrap my fingers completely around him, he is hard, so very hard. I point him toward my lips, and he gradually brings my head closer, his fingers tangled in what is left of my fancy hairstyle. I part my lips and rub them over the bulb of his cock, its rim, and as far down the shaft as I can.

I take a deep breath to accept more of him, sitting back so I can look directly up at him. I suck and slurp, spittle running out of the corner of my mouth, my eyes watering, leaving rivers of mascara running down my face like dripping paint.

"Beautiful, Lu. You know how fucking beautiful you are?" he says, rocking his hips into my face. "Grab my ass, baby. I want to feel you pull me deeper. I want you to go crazy for my dick."

I sink my self-manicured nails into the hard cheeks of his behind and pull him down my throat so hard there is no way at all that I can breathe. I hold him there as long as I can, until I feel myself getting dizzy, and then push him back out, coughing and gasping for air. Not very sexy, if you ask me, acting like such an animal with my hair and makeup destroyed, and yet he gazes down on me like I am his savior.

"Fuck yeah, baby, you know how much that turns me on?" he asks, his smile wicked. "C'mon. Get up. Go bend over the bed."

My legs are stiff from crouching for so long, so I hold his hand as I wobble. When I get there, he bends me forward until I am open for everyone to see.

"Fuck, look how wet you are," he says, swiping his fingers up my slit and rubbing my fluid on my... my behind. Actually, on my *asshole*.

Oh my god. What is he doing? I've heard about anal sex, but do people really do that? Like, normal people?

For one, how will his cock ever fit inside me, if that's what he has in mind?

But I try not to worry. These guys have never hurt me, and I know they won't now.

Max is on my one side, Rowan the other, and I guess Greyson decided it was someone else's turn. "Hey, Row, why don't you dive in here? You're the backdoor expert."

*Backdoor expert.*

That's what they call it?

"Fuck yeah, man, out of my way," he says gruffly. "I've been wanting to taste that little rosebud since I first saw it."

And when his tongue assails me, I almost fly through the roof. The sensation delivers a familiar yet different clench in my core, and I know I'll never be the same. The dirtiest of the dirty deeds, and I want it.

"Widen your legs," he growls, and when I do, he reaches around and begins to rub my little button, my *clit*.

If I am going to play their game, I am going to speak their language, no matter how strange it feels to use their naughty words.

With his tongue on my behind and fingers on my clit, I can't help but wiggle my hips like a happy little puppy. And then I feel the pressure.

Something small but firm, no doubt a finger, presses against my ass, and with more pressure, pops just inside me. It's a strange sensation, one I don't love but don't hate either, and if it makes Rowan happy, well, I can bear it for him.

The finger pulses, and in a moment, it's joined by another, stretching me bigger than I've ever been stretched before. But when they pull out, I hear the snap of a condom. I chant to myself *it will be okay, it will be okay.*

"What do you think, darlin'?" he asks. "Can I fuck you here in your pretty little ass?"

His terrible, dirty words make my nipples hard and flesh explode in goosebumps and when he moves his hand from my clit for a moment, I replace it with my own, so desperate I am for a little release.

I turn my head, resting on the bed, and see Max watching with Greyson just behind him, having opened his pants to stroke himself.

"Baby?" Rowan repeats.

I nod. "Yes, Rowan," I murmur. "Yes, yes, yes."

And then I shriek. He breaches my opening, the only way I can describe it, and it hurts but also feels good, if that is possible.

"Try and relax, baby," he says. "You'll enjoy it more if you push a bit. Bear down."

I have no idea what he means, but I squirm under him, hoping that will make it easier to get inside me, and when he does, fireworks go off all over my body, inside and out. I push back against him, wanting more, demanding more of his cock in my ass.

And he gives it to me.

When he plunges inside, it is such a shock that I arch my back, almost completely coming off the bed. He pushes me back down and thrusts in and out, drops of his sweat falling onto my back, his fingers digging at my waist.

I am a dirty girl, a nasty slut, an unrepentant sinner for letting Rowan violate my ass, but I want it to belong to him, so I writhe and scream until he is buried to the hilt. He holds himself inside me as both my pussy and ass pulse in an entirely new sort of way, one that I want to experience again. Right away, if possible, I think, as he empties himself inside me.

But it's two a.m., and we are tired. Rowan takes me to the bathroom and cleans me up, murmuring soft words, totally out of character for his gruff façade. Even though he is a prickly, unpredictable man, when it comes to me he is caring. Thoughtful. Kind. Gentle.

I'd hate to experience his other persona.

And that's when he lays the bomb on me.

"We want to take care of you, Lu. Set you up in an apartment. Give you money to spend."

It's funny, with all I've done with the guys, while I might have been conflicted, I've been able to reconcile my actions. But something about this offer doesn't sit well.

"Excuse me?" I ask, running a comb through my knotted hair.

He shrugs like people talk about things like this

all the time, standing there so unselfconscious in his nudity, beautifully muscular and strong, his now-tired cock still half-erect. "It's just what it sounds like. You'll have nothing to worry about. No more working at the club. We'll pay for your studies. Everything."

For a moment I feel like Cinderella, but then it passes and I feel plain dirty. I can't explain it, but the shame, the old shame that was my best friend and became my nemesis, bubbles back to the surface.

I don't want their money. I don't want them to take care of me. I want a relationship where we are on equal footing. Where I do as much supporting of them as they do of me.

But they don't work that way.

Which breaks my heart.

# CHAPTER SIXTEEN

## LUCI

I TAKE my time driving home, in no hurry to get there. The truth is, that while I plan to study with Charleigh today, I'm in pretty good shape for our upcoming test.

Bookkeeping suits me. It's orderly. It has rules. You always know what to do next.

*So* unlike the time I spend with Max, Rowan, and Greyson. With them, anything goes. The surprises never end.

I think I can live with a combination of the two, the certainty of bookkeeping and uncertainty of the guys. Maybe.

But the life of a bookkeeper is looking much more likely.

Not a life where three guys want to share me, who happen to also be involved in organized crime, just like all their friends and associates.

How in god's name has life put me here, in this strange union of two such different worlds? Is it some sort of test?

And if so, am I passing? Or failing?

My mood sinks as I realize my time with the guys is probably coming to an end. Gwen will never let me see them exclusively, at least not for any real length of time, and yet I can't imagine seeing any other club members. She won't bless such an arrangement, so that means my days at the club are numbered.

On the other hand, if the guys 'take care of me,' as Rowan puts it, I won't have to worry about working anywhere. But really, that would be just another job, right? And I'm not sure I want to work for these guys that way. I don't want that kind of obligation hanging over my head, always wondering if they like me for *me*, rather than the challenge of keeping me as some sort of plaything.

By the time I reach my apartment, the buzz of the previous night's excitement is pretty much extinguished. I look around the parking lot, not that anyone here pays attention to me anyway, but I want to make sure no one witnesses what is so clearly my classic morning-after 'walk of shame.'

Here I am, a massive case of bedhead, a wrinkled evening dress, carrying my shoes by the straps, wearing a ratty jacket, and trying to walk barefoot over bumpy asphalt pavement to reach the stairs to my floor.

It's a pretty gross building where I live. More like one of those old-school motels than a real apartment building. Crappy security, which is why I sleep at night with my dresser pushed in front of the door of my one-room place. But it's cheap and will continue to serve its purpose for as long as I need it to.

After fumbling with the key, I push my door open with a sigh of relief, content to be back in my crummy little home, the only place in the world that's mine and no one else's.

But as soon as I cross the threshold, I drop everything I am holding, keys included, and scream.

I'm not alone in my apartment. Not by a long shot.

And when my eyes fully adjust to the dim light, I see I've been joined by my mother, father, and the youth pastor from our church, the disgusting Sandy Rollins.

"Oh my god, what are you doing here?" I cry. "How did you get in?"

I hold onto the doorjamb, my heart pounding from the adrenaline rush.

The three of them are looking me up and down as Mom crosses her arms and presses her lips together. "Lucinda, you know better than to take the Lord's name in vain."

What? She shows up with Dad and the creepy Sandy in tow, somehow having managed to break into my home, and all she can do is scold me for saying *oh my god*?

Am I hallucinating? Please let me be hallucinating.

"How did you get in?" I repeat.

Mom helps herself to a seat on the edge of my bed. "Your landlady is very nice. She and I really hit it off, especially when I gave her one of my glazed tomato soup loaf cakes. I brought you one too."

My landlady? She bribed my landlady? That chain-smoking potty mouth, who wears too much makeup and a teased black wig every day?

Dad clears his throat. "What I want to know," he pauses to wave his hand at me, as if that sums up my admittedly slovenly appearance, "is what this is all about."

A sideways glance at Sandy—his presence is even more random than my parents—reveals his arms crossed tightly, his face wearing an expression of grave, grave concern.

If the entire situation weren't so crazy, I might actually laugh out loud.

I walk across the room—*my* room—and pull some jeans and a T-shirt out of my dresser. "I was at a party. It was late, I spent the night."

Hard to argue with that, right?

I duck into the bathroom to change my clothes. I run a comb through my hair, put on deodorant, and rejoin the three intruders.

I still don't know what they're doing there, but I do know I want them to leave.

I embrace the same sort of stern expression they're throwing my way and stare right back. "While it's nice to see you, I have studying to do. I've got a test coming up."

Sandy takes a step toward me. "Oh, for the 'course' you're taking?" he asks sarcastically, using air quotes around *course.*

What is that supposed to mean?

"Um, yeah. For the *course* I'm taking. Which I

am getting A's in, by the way," I say, reaching into my backpack and pulling out my latest A.

Sandy scoffs at the paper I wave in front of him, probably because he never earned an A in his life, narrowing his eyes as if I counterfeited the darn thing. "Lucinda, we are here today for what you might call… an intervention."

"*What?*"

"Your mother has been calling you for weeks, you haven't been getting back to her. We know you're surrounded by sinners, and we've come to get you."

I look at my parents. "Is that true? You're having Sandy do your bidding? You think I'm more likely to jump in the car and head home with you if he makes the request?"

Their non-answer answers my question.

"While we were waiting for you, Lucinda, we looked around at your… clothes, if you can call them that," Dad says, gesturing at my closet, which holds the costumes I'm sure he's referring to, "and Sandy here was able to get into your laptop and look at your history thing. You know, that shows the kinds of things you look up with Google."

They got into my *computer*?

It's all too much. Too much to absorb the absurdity and the gall of it. Too much to accept that I'm building a life away from these people, and they want to snatch it all away from me like it means nothing.

My chest hurts from the fury building in it.

"C'mon, honey," Mom says in her church lady voice, "come home with us and all will be forgiven."

*Forgiven?*

"We know you're up to something sinful, sweetie," she adds.

At least they got that part right.

"I'm not leaving. Sorry you came all this way," I say, pulling on a jacket and grabbing my backpack.

A hand lands on my arm and before I look to see who it is, my skin crawls. Because I know darn well who it is.

"Sandy, get your hands off me," I hiss, yanking my arm back.

But he's not dissuaded. In fact, he doubles down by gripping my wrist so hard I can't twist away. "Lucinda, if you would just repent and leave behind this life of sin you've adopted, all will be forgotten. In time."

Mom nods enthusiastically. "Honey, two of your old friends recently met new fellas at the church dance. The one you missed that was organized by Melanie. Who, by the way, you have not called back either."

I feel badly about that one. I do owe Melanie a return call.

But if I keep getting sucked back into the life I left, how will I be able to continue to create my new one?

"Honey," Dad starts to say, "I know you don't want to give up your exciting new life here in Chicago. You know God loves you, but when you run around wearing whorish dresses like the one you just had on—"

"JUST A MINUTE," I yell.

Oh no. I just yelled at my father.

And the world doesn't swallow me whole. Just like it didn't swallow me when I got naked for Max, Rowan, and Greyson and did... things with them.

The God my parents and Sandy talk about is vengeful and scary.

But the God I've gotten to know in recent weeks is kind and understanding. I know this. I feel it in my bones.

My new concept of God is completely and totally different from what I was brought up with and doesn't pass judgment on everything I do. No, my God is the beautiful flower growing in the crack in the sidewalk, the kindly Sam, who watches over me where I park my car at work, and the miracle of my old junker of a car continuing to chug along, getting me from one place to another even when it should have died a long time ago.

My God looks out for me. I wish my parents could see that.

Sandy, I don't really care about.

I cross my room toward the door. "You can leave now. All of you."

Sandy narrows his eyes while tears spring to my mother's, and my dad drops his head, shaking it over my being a lost cause.

When there's a knock on my door.

# CHAPTER SEVENTEEN

## LUCI

I'M SO HOPING the knock on my door is my landlady because I'm about to give her a big piece of my mind for letting anyone into my apartment without permission.

I don't care that she was lured by my mother's tomato soup cake. There is just no excuse, and I'm pretty sure what she did is illegal, to boot.

"Hey, baby."

My heart stops when I pull the door open, and strangely, I'm not sure who I'm looking at for a moment. It's like when you see someone completely out of context and *know* you know them but can't remember how.

I'm so confused. And I can't seem to move.

Or breathe.

Time has stopped, the earth is no longer spinning, and my thoughts, my speech, and my body are frozen.

Solid.

This isn't supposed to happen, my two worlds colliding.

Behind me, representing my old life, are my mother and father and Pastor Sandy.

And in front of me, right there in the flesh, I finally register, I am looking right at Max, Greyson, and Rowan.

Oh god. It's the guys.

"Since we missed you this morning, darlin'," Rowan says, "we wanted to come by and take you to lunch."

Oh no, no, no.

And questions. I have so many questions.

But all I can do is mumble the stupidest one. "H… how do you know where I live?"

The guys look at each other with small smiles.

Oh. Okay. Right.

Got it.

Max leans against the doorjamb, apparently unable to see into the dimly lit room behind me. "You know, baby, we were a little worried we scared you off with our proposal last night. Knowing Rowan," he says with a laugh, "he fucked up the whole conversation.

I shut my eyes, as if doing so will backspace to a spot where I can start all over.

But when I open them, my three hot lovers are still there, and someone behind me clears their throat.

These opposite ends of my life—the old and the new, the one in front of me and the one behind— have no business overlapping. The connection could be lethal.

This isn't supposed to happen.

But then, I guess I wasn't supposed to leave my hometown, come to Chicago, study bookkeeping, or dress up at the club and play with three gorgeous mafia men.

Oops.

Was it inevitable?

Without looking, I know my mother is at my side. I don't see her or hear her and yet I know she's there.

"WHO are these men, Lucinda?" she shrills.

Max peels himself from the doorjamb and extends his hand. "You must be Lu's mother. I can totally see the resemblance," he says with a big smile.

Oh god, oh god, oh god.

This is the calm before the storm. And this storm is going to be very, very bad.

Mom takes a step back. "LU?" she spits, glaring at me before she zeroes in on Max. "Her name is *Lucinda*, young man, and I'd like to know who in the devil you are. And your *friends* here."

She wedges herself between me and the guys, and while my first instinct is to shrink back and let the adults fight it out, I remember that's how the old Luci would do things.

The one I left behind.

I elbow my way right back to front and center. "Excuse me, Mom, but these gentlemen are my friends."

Realization is beginning to wash over the guys' faces. They know to tread carefully.

I guess in their line of business, they learn to read people pretty well.

Rowan stretches to his full height and looks over my mom's shoulder. "Lu's got other visitors, too," he says, looking at Dad and Sandy.

Mom steps aside as if to show she has backup. The guys enter my apartment, such as it is, and look around in shock. I'm not completely sure whether they are more surprised by my living conditions, my visitors, or something else.

Greyson takes up right beside me. "Lu, are these your parents, honey?" he asks.

And instead of flinching, I straighten my shoulders and lift my chin. "Yes, Grey. My mother and father, and that over there is Sandy Rollins."

Sandy takes a step forward, clearly unaware of what he's up against. "That's *Pastor* Sandy. Lucinda, you know better."

The contempt in his voice is revolting. And unforgivable. I don't care how he feels about me or these guys, whom he doesn't even know. The way he speaks to people is intended to manipulate and terrorize. And I'm over that shit.

I scowl at him. "Sandy, shut the *hell* up," I snarl.

His eyes widen, but I'm done with him. Just done.

"You're a disgusting little perv, Sandy. Everyone knows how you jerk off to porn, not to mention all the times you've grabbed my ass over the years. Don't you go acting better than everyone else because you surely are NOT!"

Dad is speechless, but then he's always let Mom do the talking for the two of them.

I turn back to the guys. "My parents showed up here with the intention of taking me back home. They thought bringing Pastor Creepy would help them make the case."

The guys indifferently size up Sandy, then turn back to me, unimpressed.

"Well, are you going?" Max asks. "Because it doesn't exactly look like you want to take us up on our offer."

Mom gasps. Because of course.

But I ignore her because her vote no longer counts. She only wants the *idea* of me in her life. She'll never accept the real me.

She never has.

"I… it's not what I want, Max," I say softly. "I don't want to be your mistress—"

But I don't get to finish.

"YOU ARE A WHORE, LUCINDA BRAX-TON!" Sandy bellows.

Rowan rolls his eyes. Sighing, he takes a step toward Sandy, and smacks him across the face with his open palm.

Then he rejoins the conversation like nothing ever happened. Meanwhile, I look over my shoulder to see Sandy on the ground, cradling his jaw, his pride clearly hurt more than anything else.

He's lucky he didn't get Rowan's closed fist.

"You… you must repent, Lucinda," he hollers from the floor, one arm outstretched, as if he could only reach me, he might be able to save my doomed soul.

"Buddy, could you shut the fuck up?" Rowan yells.

And because Sandy continues bellowing his fire and brimstone absurdities, Max and Greyson pick him up with a hand under each arm, escort him out of my apartment, and close the door to shut out his racket.

That leaves my mom and dad, who stand there, mouths open.

"What is it you want, baby?" Max asks.

Ah. Could I say it? Dare I say it?

"I… want there to be something real between us. Not some sort of transactional arrangement."

Dad clears his throat and taps me on the shoulder. "Honey, I think we'll be leaving now." He kisses me on the forehead and leaves, dragging Mom, who won't even make eye contact with me.

Before he pulls the door closed behind them, he gives me a sad smile. "We don't approve of what you're doing, honey, but we will always love you."

The sadness in both his eyes and words contribute to the already-huge lump in my throat, and the resulting tears in my own eyes are not lost on the guys.

The door *clicks* after Dad. The sound is so quiet and so, so sad.

Like something died.

The loss of a pretend existence, where I'm my parents' nice church-going, god-fearing daughter, is something I thought I'd be happy about. Saying goodbye to the old, conflicted, tortured *me*. But I never considered how it might hurt them. No matter how wrong they are, I've never felt vindictive toward them.

What the hell do I do now? I can't go back home, not that I want to, and I am certain my days at Club Sin are numbered. Sure, I've got some money in the bank for the first time in my life, but that will only last so long.

Maybe Charleigh will have some ideas. Her dad owns a shop, after all.

"Sweetie," Rowan says, pulling me out of my thoughts with an arm around my shoulders, "you never told us about this part of your upbringing."

No, I hadn't. Would *they* have told *me*, had they come from the same place?

"I didn't want you to know. I don't want anyone to know. Ever. You wouldn't either. Can you understand that?" I ask.

He nods slowly. "Yeah. Yeah, I can."

"Now you know my biggest secret. If you feel the need to run away from me as fast as you can, I'll understand," I say with a pathetic laugh.

It's beyond me why these guys are interested in

me anyway, and I'm sure their attraction is tenuous at best. Sure, we had plenty of fun in the sack, but now that they know who I am and what I come from, I'm sure they're even less interested. Men in the mafia—or syndicate, as they call it—don't need someone like me around.

Max frowns at me. "What? Run away? Are you kidding? Look at all you've accomplished. You've escaped a tyrannical upbringing. You know how big a deal that is?"

Um, yeah.

But I just shrug. I'm tired. So tired.

"Look," Max says, "why don't you let us take you back to Greyson's? He's got the biggest house, and you'll be the most comfortable there. No strings attached, sweetie. No sex or anything… unless you want it, of course. You can just chill there as long as you want, or until you come down from this… shitshow."

He pauses long enough to throw me that dimpled smile.

Damn him.

He's so hard to say no to. All the guys are.

And it might be my last opportunity to spend time with them before everything starts to go south.

"Bring your books," he continues, "so you can

study. We'll get you something to eat, and you can chill in peace."

After the drama of being confronted by my parents and Pastor Pervert, I have to admit Max's offer sounds nice. It's been a rough day and it's not even noon yet.

It figures, just when I'm getting my feet under me, settled on solid ground, something has to come along and upset it all. I guess life is just like that.

"Okay, guys. Let's go."

# CHAPTER EIGHTEEN

## LUCI

SQUIRRELED AWAY in a far corner of Greyson's house, I close my laptop after my Zoom call with Charleigh. She's cool with the fact that I wasn't up for the drive to meet her in person, and to be honest, we actually got more done in our virtual study session.

We are both going to ace our exams. I can feel it.

It's a nice boost after what happened earlier in the day. Although it's a minor miracle I could get any work done, anyway.

Now I need to focus on next steps. Just when I am about to write down all my options, limited though the list may be, there is a soft knock at the door of the room where I'm hanging out, having time to myself.

"Yes?" I call.

The door opens a crack and Max sticks his head through. "Can I join you for a minute?"

I gather up the books and papers I spread out on the bed where I was studying, and make a spot for him to sit on.

The crazy, curly hair he usually has pulled back into a ponytail is loose, a soft contrast to the sharp, masculine angles of his face. As is his usual habit, he rakes his fingers through his hair, pulling it back off his forehead, only for it to snap back into place.

My god, he is cute.

"I think maybe you need a barrette or something," I tease, pointing at his unruly curls.

He grabs my hand and smiles. "I think maybe you are right. How was studying?"

"Great. I think we're really well prepared. I'm hoping for another A."

The A grades make me feel good. I can't lie. Even thinking about them makes me feel good. As if anything is possible, and that I'll eventually find my way.

I started over once before and I'm sure I can do

it again. Club Sin isn't a long-term solution, anyway.

Right?

"Lu, we guys have something on our minds, and well, I'm the one who wants to talk to you about it."

"Okay."

I've learned anything can happen when the guys want to have a 'talk.' But I'm not nervous this time. I want to hear what they have to say.

"We didn't mean to… insult you by offering to take care of you. You see, what we want, what we are hoping for, is much more than having you at our sexual beck and call. We want *you*. This is real —not Club Sin dress-up games. As much fun as they are," he adds.

For the second time today, I'm speechless. I look at Max and open my mouth to say something, and have no idea where to start.

They like me, they do, and the problem is, if I'm honest with myself and really think about all the possibilities around me, this is what I want. I'm growing attached to them—scratch that, I already *am* attached to them—and I'm just now letting myself acknowledge that truth. I couldn't have done it before. It was too risky, and I was too afraid.

I get my voice back. "I... I'm falling for you guys. You need to know that."

Max tilts his head, and as my words sink in, a smile slinks across his face. "So here's the thing," he says, "we are designing one gigantic house for the three of us and would love to set you up in a bedroom in the center of it. You know, since you're going to be the center of our lives."

My heart soars. I know I have a ton of challenges ahead, not least of which is understanding the guys' work and how the hell three guys share one woman. But I'm game if they are.

"You know, Max," I say, "you told me once you thought you'd die alone. That no woman would want to be with a guy like you, who's in your line of work."

"Yeah. I did say that." He presses his lips together. Maybe regretting his words?

"Well, I guess I just proved you wrong."

We burst out laughing, and seconds later we're joined by Rowan and Greyson.

"Sounds like you sealed the deal, man," Greyson says, offering Max a high-five.

Rowan jumps onto the bed and pulls me to him. "Good work, Max. You didn't fuck it up," he laughs.

Max faux-punches him.

"So, guys, one request," I say.

They turn to me, their faces serious.

"Anything you want, baby."

"Your wish is my command."

"Just name it, darling."

"When can we go back to Room 21?"

---

*EPILOGUE*

*Seems I said goodbye a little too quickly. It took some time, but my parents rattled the universe and beyond when they called me. Actually, they didn't just call, although that was a surprise in itself, but they also invited me to dinner. At their house.*

*With the guys.*

*To say I never thought I'd see the day when my parents wanted to spend time with me apart from reiterating how I was a sinner destined for the depths of hell, is an understatement of proportion even bigger than my affection for the guys.*

*And that's saying a lot.*

*That I've fallen for them—Max, Rowan, and Greyson—is no secret. But it doesn't begin to describe my feelings. I am a completely new person, formed in part by my quest to be something other than what I was originally destined for, and especially due to the guys'* influence. When it comes down to it, they get a lot of credit for the woman I have become. And continue to become. They shaped me. Created me. Molded me.

Some might say that's creepy.

I say it's hot.

For as long as I can remember, I wanted to escape the suffocating dreariness of my surroundings. And I did. I actually, truly did. But not all by myself.

Honestly, I had the help of a lot of people.

I guess the first person I have to thank is Melanie, my bestie from home. While our lives have wildly diverged, her support of me has never wavered, not even for a moment. She sees me. She's always seen me. And while my choices are not ones she would have made, she understands why I've done what I have. She wants me to do more of it, too. She wants me to take on what she can't even fathom, because she knows that's best for me.

And she wants only the best for me.

Maybe someday I can show her there's more out there for her, too.

Cripes, when I think about it, I also owe kudos to my less-than-nice Club Sin boss, Gwen. Her treating me as not much more than a walking ATM taught me I need to look out for myself, because most people won't. She never really gave a crap about me, or anyone, for that matter. Behind that façade of smiles is nothing *other than cold eyes and a cold heart. Kind of a sad way to go through life.*

*My study buddy and partner-in-crime, Charleigh, is like a blessing sent from the gods. I wouldn't have made it through bookkeeping without her. We egged each other on to study harder and do better, and ended up being the course's star students. A first for both of us.*

*While her dad runs a scruffy pawn shop, her upbringing wasn't that different from mine. She was sheltered in the name of religion like me, and is now just emerging from under it. She might even be ahead of me on the journey, although she hasn't ended up with three guys like I have.*

*Although I think she might like it, should it happen. I'm keeping my eyes open for her.*

*The most credit for my transformation goes to the guys, starting with my darling Max. After resolving himself to the life of a single man, he's learned someone can love him, and that someone is me. I love to tease him about this while I brush out his long hair and experiment with his pony tails and man buns. He always takes them back out because mine are too 'girlish,' as he says.*

*But I'm going to keep trying until I've got it right.*

*My grouchy Rowan, who is the kindest, most sensitive person I know, still wakes up from nightmares every now and then, haunted by witnessing his father's* death. His scars will never go away, but it's my hope that with the love we have, his nightmares will cease, at least a little over time. I comfort him when he calls out in his sleep, but he often pushes me away. That's his prickly side. I'm working on that, too.

The quiet Greyson has been in charge of building the new house for all of us, and has included me in all the decisions, especially those related to my 'wing' of the building. I get to choose everything I want for my room there, and it's going to be a dream come true, thanks to all the great ideas I get from Pinterest. The best part is the closet, which has one long wall for hanging things, and the other for shelving everything else. There's a dresser in the middle that holds undies and things like that, and my growing jewelry collection is housed in a couple pretty boxes on top.

Greyson seems to know a lot of people in the construction business, because this project is coming together pretty fast. Actually, he knows a lot of people in a lot of businesses.

I keep my questions to myself. I don't really want to know how or why.

Last, I can't forget the multitude of kindnesses I've received from my dear parking lot attendant, Sam. He was like my guardian angel for so long. He still is, actually, although I rarely park in his lot anymore since I no longer work at the club. I just attend now with the guys *as a member, and we always get dropped off at the door. I miss seeing him but I always ask the guys to drive by his lot so I can check to see that he's okay. He still seems to be dispensing free advice to anyone who will listen. And anyone who listens is better for it.*

*All these people have helped me become the person I am. I'd be nothing without them.*

*And yes, my parents actually did invite the guys and me for a dinner last week. At first I intended to decline the invite, but Greyson talked me into accepting.*

*My mother was pretty quiet, although I have to give her credit for putting on a great meal. My father was the more talkative one, honestly curious about the guys, and surprisingly uninterested in our 'unique' arrangement. I think he was just trying not to think about how unusual it is, and was really trying to get a sense of what the guys were all about and whether or not they really seemed committed to me. Of course, when Dad asked them about their work, they answered vaguely, but clearly enough to satisfy him.*

*Did my parents still think I was destined for the depths of hell? Probably. But they were still interested in my well-being. They hadn't completely written me off. Which was a big step for them.*

*Sandy, the creepy pastor, was sent away someplace, where, I do not know. Nor do I care. When the parish found out how handsy he was with young, female* churchgoers, he was driven out of town so fast he didn't know what hit him.

As soon as I got home that night after dinner with my parents, I thanked the universe for giving me everything I never knew I wanted, and everything I needed. A career, the belief in myself, and the love of three men. They might be kinky as shit and earn their living outside the bounds of the law, but I adore everything about each of them and am so happy that something or someone blessed me with them.

I'm not clear what the future holds for me, but I'm pretty sure with the guys at my side we can accomplish anything that comes our way.

After all, I am their plaything.

Now and forever.

Did you like Luci's story in *Plaything for the Mafia?*
Check out the sexy, steamy
*Her Bratva Christmas.*

**This Christmas, bullets will fly and my heart will be on the line.**

As a party planner, I watch the rich and powerful glitterati of New York enjoy the fruits of my back-breaking labor.

Caviar? Check. Champagne? Check. Flowers imported from the far corners of the earth? Check.

And when it's all done, I go home.

Alone.

If I'm lucky, with leftover food from the caterer.

But a Christmas Eve party shootout changes everything.

Three handsome men with guns kill everyone...

Except me.

One minute, I'm a hard-working party planner.
The next, I'm a prisoner.
These men claim I'm in danger. And the only way to protect me is by abduction.
So, I end up kidnapped by the terrifying, dangerous Bratva, New York's powerful crime syndicate.
And yet, just beneath the surface of my fear is a blazing, unsettling attraction.
When I wake on Christmas morning at their hide-out, everything changes.
These violent killers have a soft side.
Lavishing me with attention and gifts.
Until, all I want for Christmas is—them.

Download it now.

AND... find all Mika Lane books here

---

Ready to step into the next Club Sin fantasy?
Room Twenty-three by Alexa Jordan is next

# CLUB SIN: CHICAGO

🔑 **Club Sin: New York** took your breath away. Now visit **Club Sin: Chicago** for more play sessions. 🔑

Fantasies are meant to come true and the men of **Club Sin: Chicago** will see to your every kinky desire. We'll take you inside to a forbidden place where you'll find love and pleasure with multiple hot men in these Reverse Harem stories. Can you handle the heat?

**10 rooms, 10 fantasies...**
**Which door will you step through?**

🩶 Check out the series and order your copies today! 🩶

Room Two by Penelope Wylde

Room Four by Ember Davis

Room Seven by Tamrin Banks

Room Nine by Kameron Claire

Room Eleven by Layne Daniels

Room Fifteen by Elyse Kelly

Room Seventeen by Penelope Wylde

Room Eighteen by Ember Davis

Room Twenty-One by Mika Lane

Room Twenty-Three by Alexa Jordan

# ABOUT THE AUTHOR

I'm USA TODAY bestselling contemporary romance author Mika Lane, and am all about bringing you sexy, sassy stories with imperfect heroines and the bad-a*s dudes they bring to their knees. And I have a special love for romance with multiple guys because why should we have to settle for just one hunky man?

Please join my Insider Group and be the first to hear about giveaways, sales, pre-orders, ARCs, and most importantly, a free sexy short story: http://mikalane.com/join-mailing-list/.

Writing has been a passion of mine since, well, forever (my first book was *The Day I Ate the Milky-way*, a true fourth-grade masterpiece). These days, steamy romance, both dark and funny, gives purpose to my days and nights as I create worlds and characters who defy the imagination. I live in magical Northern California with my own hand-some alpha dude, sometimes known as Mr. Mika Lane, and two devilish cats named Chuck and Murray. These three males also defy my imagina-tion from time to time.

A lover of shiny things, I've been known to try new recipes on unsuspecting friends, find hiding places so I can read undisturbed, and spend my last dollar on a plane ticket somewhere.

I'll always promise you a hot, sexy romp with kick-ass but imperfect heroines, and some version of a modern-day happily ever after.

I LOVE to hear from readers when I'm not dreaming up naughty tales to share. Join my Insider Group so we can get to know each other better http://mikalane.com/join-mailing-list, or contact me here: https://mikalane.com/contact.